The Freeze

A Novel

RON DEBOER

ISBN: 1973770288
ISBN 13: 9781973770282
Library of Congress Control Number: 2017914278
CreateSpace Independent Publishing Platform
North Charleston, South Carolina

For my wife Helen and our children Jeneen and Jason

AUTHOR'S NOTE

Before becoming a soldier, I was a ditch digger. I shared the trench with ancient Hibernian laborers. They taught me the proper use of a shovel, to swing a pick and discretely sip a brew from a glove while standing on Madison Avenue. They were gifted storytellers, who spun their tales with a gritty oral prose. I was fortunate to be their audience. A rifle went on to replace the shovel. Laborers and soldiers, men I came to know. My hope is, the reader will hear their voices on these pages and cherish their memory as I do.

1

NEW YORK CITY. CHRISTMASTIME.
"SILENT NIGHT" AND A DEAF - MUTE NUN.

Flann struck a match and suspiciously eyed the flame that danced around the bowl of his corncob pipe. Not a soul could recall seeing him without the pipe, and so the pipe became part of his face, a friend to the mole peeking out from his bushy eyebrow.

He was a seanchai, a storyteller, the finest in Washington Heights and the mayor of Shiloh, his own magical kingdom in the north of Ireland, a hidden hamlet, where marvelous things happened.

Butterflies spoke and mules laughed and where the fish left their ponds and pranced down McGowan Lane to tease a cow owned by a farmer named Gaynor. His old friend, Jack Curry, said the words came to the ear gift-wrapped when Flann McFarland spun a story. Flann was the Super of 650 and resided in the cellar with the coal he shoveled and the furnace he stoked. But Flann believed he was and conducted himself like the captain of a ship, responsible for everything and everyone aboard.

The children gathered on the stoop of 650 in the summertime, after the simmering asphalt of 177th Street cooled lured by moss-scented words that floated upon a whimsical breeze that strayed eastward from a tranquil Hudson River, and journeyed with Flann to Shiloh.

One thing was certain, it was not summer. It was the winter of 1962, the cruelest winter anyone could remember. "Bein' so cold the lawyers have their hands in their own pockets." That is what Flann said, and because he said it, the children on the street said it and soon everyone was saying it.

Everyone, except for attorney Brian Kelly whose storefront law office was down the block from 650 and across the street from the High Spot Bar, a waiting room for many of his clients. Kelly himself, found no humor in it at all, nor did he appreciate Flann's demeaning summer forecast. " 'Tis so hot the lawyers are taking the shirts off their own backs."

The people christened the frigid air The Freeze, and it was in its third week. Anything that could freeze froze, not only fingers and toes and the tips of noses, but also every lock on every store on both Broadway and Saint Nicholas Avenue. The shivering merchants set to work scraping frost formed by hissing steam pipes from their windows and hoped that a pedestrian, as stiff as a Popsicle, might pause and purchase a Christmas gift. The warmest sweaters ever knitted were neatly folded and stacked in Donohue's Irish gift store. If a pair of penny loafers, desert boots, or saddle shoes was on the Christmas list, all a shopper need do was gaze in the window of Tom McCann's, which was right next door.

The Freeze created a frozen ache shared by the entire city. Coal-fueled furnaces were breaking down causing testy crowds to form outside of City Hall insisting that the mayor take action and repair the furnaces when the landlords failed to act, which was often. But there was no snow on the ground and not a flake was in the forecast and that troubled the children huddled in the hallway of 650. Everyone understood Flann's explanation for the lack of winter precipitation, which he explained in a way that did not require weather maps.

"For sure the snow, 'tis frozen in the clouds," Flann said as he made his way up the stairs, holding his pipe with one hand and using the banister as a crutch with the other.

"Are ya not rememberin' my tellin' ya about the nun?" he asked the children.

"The nun without a name," replied Joey Carlo. The eleven-year-old lived on what Flann dubbed the Delicious Fourth Floor. The aroma was a year-round gift that seeped under the door of apartment forty-four, home to Mrs. Carlo's kitchen.

Flann had competed with the Italians for the basic things in life since the day he arrived on Ellis Island in New York harbor on a muggy July day 1900. For a job. For a place to live. For a bit of dignity. He had spent forty-five years in the trench, a laborer for the electric company, working in the SSS Division which stood for Sub-Surface Structures. But the men, Irish and Italian alike, called it, "Shovel Shit and Shovel."

Hunger permitted Flann to pardon Joey Carlo's Italian family tree. Hunger was his dance partner for life and had shadowed him since the day he was born. Hunger became the playmate that replaced Tomas, the twin brother his mother told him died one hour after they were born. It never mattered how many cans of chicken soup he stashed under his cot or in his closet. The pain of hunger remained tattooed on Flann's soul like the faded shamrock on his forearm.

The slab of baked lasagna wrapped in aluminum foil and lowered by Joey from his fire escape to Flann erased a multitude of insults uttered between Irish and Italian laborers in the trench when the foreman turned his back. Flann treasured Italian food, but for reasons closer to his stomach than his heart, he never admitted.

To ensure his class was paying attention, Flann started with a pop quiz. "And let me be askin' ya if she might be heard singin' a Christmas carol?"

"Not a word. She was born deaf and dumb," answered Sean O'Leary from apartment twenty-two. The Freeze had etched a fiery red into his porcelain cheeks that not even a night in a warm bed could erase.

"What's one to do with a non singin' nun? What name might she take or what use could she have been to Reverend Mother Ruth who was known for havin' the finest choir in the north of Ireland?" asked Flann.

"It's not right to call a person dumb because they can't speak," said Katherine Dunn, called Kate by everyone except for her mother.

Editorializing comments from the daughter of detective Liam Dunn were common. Everyone knew that, especially Flann McFarland, formerly of Belfast.

"As certain as there is water in ice, a burden to herself 'tis what Kate Dunn will become," muttered Flann peering over the banister at his congregation. Flann was not about to jeopardize the five remaining teeth in his mouth by bearing down on his pipe so he removed it and made a horrid face, twisting his jaw and tugging on his chin.

"I'm sure she can think. Thinking and talking are different. Right Flann?" Kate drove him to the edge of insanity with her questions which were more a statement of her own version of the very thing Flann was attempting to say.

Flann could not avoid what was happening. He knew not every handshake would lead to friendship, just as he understood not every child would be able to forsake realty and escape to Shiloh. Before Kate Larry Cohen could not make the trek. The ten-year-old probed everything.

Flann could barely contain his joy when Larry announced his parents were joining the exodus to Long Island, starting a new life in Hicksville, where a man named Levitt created Levittown, his own magical kingdom.

Flann pacified himself by focusing on Thursday, his Sabbath, his day of rest and the day he relished above all others. On Thursday, Kate Dunn would be absent from Flann's hallway and present at Sister Evangeline's confirmation class, for sixteen blessed weeks.

Kate would receive the sacred Rite of Confirmation. Last year a stir had arisen when the auxiliary bishop from Brooklyn had arrived. Bishop Carlos Mendez, born in Santo Domingo. Twenty years a priest and five years a bishop. His complexion resembled a Colombian coffee bean and that took the parents by surprise. He was fluent in five languages and his English was flawless. Yet, when he spoke, his accent left no doubt concerning his Latin American roots. When Bishop Mendez greeted the Confirmation candidates and addressed the congregation of proud parents, he announced that he was the former Dean of Students at Notre Dame.

No one anticipated what many decreed a miracle. Suddenly, the bishop became as white as the snow that Flann's own congregation hoped would arrive in time for Christmas. It became a delightful and magnificent day. Everyone wanted to have a picture taken with the former Dean of Students at the home of the Fighting Irish. Only coach Knute Rockne himself, standing in front of Incarnation Church in Washington Heights would have made for a holier day. But there was no chance the former dean would confirm Kate. Shortly after last year's jubilant celebration the Pope beckoned him to Rome. It came as no surprise; everyone understood the Vatican needed a man like Bishop Mendez.

■ ■ ■

From where Kate called her pew, on the second step from the top of the landing below Flann, she could see apartment twenty-one. If it had not been Christmastime, no one would have noticed the door. It would have been identical to the other doors in 650, the color of rotting strawberries, a choice more appropriate for doors guarding prison sink closets.

"Even in the greenish forest there can always be found a barren tree." That is what Flann said about the door to apartment twenty-one, a door that lacked any sort of holiday exaltation. But no one was thinking about the color of the twenty-four apartment doors within 650 or the poor choice of color made decades earlier. Happiness would triumph over gloom, even though for some it was a short reprieve, because it was Christmas week in Washington Heights and that meant lugging holiday treasure chests from under beds and off cluttered closet shelves.

The day before, door twenty-one had cracked opened. Kate caught sight of a hand with a road map of purple veins securing the door's chain. She had told no one about the chain or the hand, not even her best friend Mary Garvey, with whom she shared nearly everything. A cold plagued Mary every year which arrived precisely on Halloween and lasted until Easter. Her nose never stopped running and for that reason Kevin Kramer, who lived on the fifth floor and whom everyone shunned, crowned her Mary, Queen of Snots.

The day apartment twenty-one became occupied was a mystery. The moving truck came and left before the milkman arrived. The usual cardboard boxes, flattened and used by the youngest children to slide down the stairs, were nowhere in sight.

People assumed that whatever possessions were inside apartment twenty-one had arrived in the brown burlap bags with black stenciled letters that read "Idaho Potatoes" and became the shades on the windows that faced the street. Flann calculated that the bags were once home to one hundred and twenty pounds of potatoes. The burlap sacks guarded against prying eyes and allowed only the faintest of light to escape, like the dying moments of a candle flickering within a jack- o'- lantern.

All that was certain was the name Grimes on the brass mailbox in the lobby. The only person Kate observed leaving the apartment was a woman whose attire was a successful attempt to conceal her identity and protect her from whatever an unexpected weather event might present.

No one knew the color of the woman Grimes' hair or if she even had a hair on her head because her head was wrapped in a black turban no matter the season or the time of day. Heart shaped sunglasses, the kind won at carnivals with red lenses and pink frames covered half of her forehead and most of her cheeks.

Grimes, wrapped in a tan raincoat, walked close to the buildings in spurts of ten cautious steps, as if she were a mouse caught in the open. Her red rubber boots slapped her shins creating a clapping sound that applauded her movement. Flann said the Grimes woman was a dwarf. "A foot shorter than five feet and generous I'm bein'." He thought Kate might be a dwarf of some sort but kept that to himself. If Detective Dunn heard a word spoken about the height of his daughter, it would mean trouble for Flann.

Kate was short there was no debating that. An unspoken concern lived with the Dunn family in apartment thirty-one that Kate might not grow another inch and she hadn't in two years. The pencil marks on the dumbwaiter door had once served as a persistent reminder of that.

The previous year, Colleen Dunn had reconsidered having her three children step forward for measurement taking. When the landlord, whom Flann called, "the Lord of the Land," sent the painters, she no longer taped a page from the *Journal American* over the marks that shielded them from a fresh coat of yellow semi-gloss. Kate's brother Rory, a sophomore at All Hallows High School, was moving along fine concerning issues of height. He was the best linebacker on the junior varsity football team and could have played varsity if the rules allowed.

Measurement Day was unbearable for Kate. She knew the hated line on the dumbwaiter would not move because Mary had been secretly measuring Kate every other week. Worse, Kate's little brother, Danny, was growing half an inch an hour, or so it seemed to Kate.

Rory and Danny ignored the forbidden topic when they returned home from school. Not a word came from Liam as he spun the chamber on his service revolver, letting the rounds fall into his palm.

His silence continued as he studied the dumbwaiter door while locking the cabinet above the refrigerator where he stored the weapon and ammunition. The marks would remain entombed, and never resurrected. Kate remained convinced, that if things did not change, her life would be profoundly different. To compensate for what she feared would be a life of *smallness*, she envisioned herself on a grand scale, grander than anyone, outside of her own mind could fathom, not even Mary Queen of Snots.

■ ■ ■

Flann puffed on his pipe, allowing time for the children to pull up a mental stool and rest in his world while he explained how the Nameless Novice, found herself cured on the snowy Christmas Eve following her sixteenth birthday. It was the work of the Straw Spiders who resided in the convent of The Sisters of the Poor in Belfast. They crept into her ear, with a splinter from Saint Patrick's staff dipped in a magical blend of bee's honey mixed with unicorn milk.

"A holy Q-Tip!" exclaimed Joey, picking small balls of lint from a morsel of Turkish Taffy pulled from his pocket.

Everyone except Flann began to laugh. A draw on his pipe sent a fresh cloud down the stairwell. Like blessed incense, Cherry Blend tobacco filled the air and the noses of Flann's audience as he continued with his story.

"The nun's only complaint after her curin' was the difficulty she was havin' fallin' asleep. The nun's hearin' was so improved that the sound of the moths flutterin' their wings was keepin' her awake."

Danny sat on his sister Kate's lap holding one of last year's five Christmas presents. It had become his most prized possession; a blue-and-white balsa wood glider he named Dart. Scotch tape held together one of Dart's wings after it crashed into a two-foot replica of Godzilla. Danny paused from navigating the plane around Kate's head pondering the sound of fluttering moth wings.

"After the nun was cured, she began to sing and it was only proper for her to take the name of Sister Angelica for she truly did have the voice of an angel. Now, we're all havin' our own idea as to what heaven might be lookin' like but from the day she sang her first note twas never a doubt as to what heaven sounded like. For as long as the nun lived, even past the age of eighty-three she held on to her voice. And the people of Ireland were glad for it." Flann gave the pipe three solid raps on the marble step, ending the story as if he were a judge banging down a gavel.

With Christmas seven days away, Flann considered it fitting to put to rest any misconceptions there might be, concerning the history linked with a part of Christmas close to every Christian heart, especially during the time of year for hymn singing and humming. Flann wove a page from a history book he had written into every story. His ability to juggle facts rivaled that of the best politician. Flann supposed, if people were enjoying what they were hearing it did not matter if truth found itself mingling with a dainty fib.

"Even the Anglicans," Flann began the lesson, "could be heard singin' our hymn." According to Flann, Cornelius Moore, a shepherd from County Cork, wrote the most cherished hymn of Christmas, "Silent Night" during the potato famine.

"A pitiful attempt to bring a note of joy to the hearts of the Irish while the British fiddled away with full stomachs," explained Flann. It made perfect sense. Everyone knew that the tenders of flocks played a significant role in the very first Christmas.

"'*Silent Night*' began as a poem written by Moore in 1845." Flann's words became as solemn as a priest did leading the rosary.

"When he recited the words, his sheep slipped off to a deep sleep. It calmed them so that the shepherds of Ireland, Protestant and Catholic alike, were speaking his words during shearin' season. The sheep couldn't wait to have their wool taken from their backs."

"Like the lawyer's shirts in summer!" said Sean.

"Exactly. And I hope the rest of ya are paying attention as well as Sean O'Leary is," proclaimed Flann. But the real magic occurred when Flann introduced Damien Moore in the tale, Cornelius' cousin, who lived in County Kerry and learned to play the flute, on his own, at the age of seven.

"A sorry excuse for a school with not even a desk for the teacher and no thought of a music class, but it wouldn't be stoppin' Damien. By the time he reached the age of seventeen years, his fate twas sealed. The hauntin' sound of his flute drew crowds to the fields of every village he visited and, sadly, caught the attention of none other than Sir Edward Davies, the despised Earl of Cambridge. A black hearted man, a master craftsman when it came to swindlin' an acre of fine Irish land," said Flann, close to weeping.

Billows of pipe smoke filled the stairwell. Flann was at his best when the story was finding its way to another brutal act orchestrated by the loathed English.

"Havin' the poem written by Cornelius Moore was one thing," Flann said pulling himself to his feet with the aid of the bannister. Forty-five years of hard labor had left his back a wretched mess. Every swing of the pick and shovel full of dirt revisited him morning, noon and night. He shifted his frail frame from left foot to right, in a dance as natural to Flann as a mother rocking her baby on her hip.

"Two years later in 1847, Damien put the words to music and the Earl of Cambridge sprung his sick plan against the two Moore boys," said Flann, with one solid rap of his pipe on the banister. He slowly lowered himself back on to the marble step and adjusted the pipe in his mouth.

"Twas okay for the lowly shepherds to be utterin' a poem among themselves, but once it twas set to music and spread from church to church and county to county and with the Moore boys fame growin' and everyone takin' up the singin' of Silent Night it twas clear in the worthless mind of Sir Edward Davies that something had to be done to bring the merriment to an end."

The years in the trench had twisted Flann's spine like the three-cent salted pretzel he enjoyed while sipping on a pint of Guinness. The hearing in his left ear was long gone, stolen by air hammers, but for some unknown reason, the hearing in his right ear, what he called his, "hearin' ear," remained. And for the moment, he regretted it.

"A German wrote 'Silent Night.'" Kate's whispered words landed in Flann's hearin' ear like pebbles tossed in a pond by a bored angler, a splash barely heard, creating ripples so slight as to not waken a napping dragonfly on the water's surface.

Flann had mastered a full deck of voices he could beckon to enhance a story. It might be the high pitched shrill of an annoying Droll, or the raspy voice of Solomon the toad, who tricked Joel the rabbit into sharing his hole in the Doyle vegetable patch on Abby Lane.

Not far from the small hamlet where Flann lived until he reached thirteen and where his twin died at the age of one hour, followed by his Ma and Da that very same miserable of 1887.

Flann drew the Solomon Toad card. "Am I hearin'-no, I'm just thinkin' I'm hearin' aye-yes, that's what it's bein' - words floatin' from the direction of Miss Kate Dunn. And now I have to be askin' myself why I'm not feelin' at all surprised."

Danny piloted Dart over his lap, failing in every attempt to land. He repeated Kate's whisper, loud enough to eliminate any doubt Flann might be having about the voice in his head.

"A German wrote 'Silent Night,'" said Danny.

"A German sheppard! Wait a minute! Isn't that a dog?" asked Joey as he began to do a respectable imitation of a yelping canine that caused his Turkish taffy to fall from his mouth, splattering on the marble floor.

"Stop!" Flann erupted, "And don't you be utterin' another sinful word Mr. Carlo for sure I won't be havin' ya undo over a hundred years of sacred Irish history nor tarnish the memory of Cornelius and Damien Moore who were hanged by the order of Davies on the trumped-up charges that they were conspiring to assassinate the First Lord of the Admiralty!"

"It's just that in the hymnal," Kate said, in her best matter-of-fact-voice, as she put Danny's hat back on his head, "it read Germany, Franz Xaver Gruber 1818."

Flan regained his wits, remembering he was in a conversation with the daughter of Liam Dunn, a persuasive man in his own right and the owner of a gold police shield.

"And so, is that what it reads in the hymnal?"

Flann had returned to a gentle brogue. Over half a century of tobacco in every form had sanded his vocal chords and now the words became more like wren feathers tied into flies, tempting children like plump springtime trout. Kate watched the door chain on apartment twenty-one push back against its last link.

"Yes. Germany. 1818," said Kate, standing Danny up on his feet.

"And now, let me be askin' ya a question, if ya wouldn't be mindin', " said Flann.

"Not at all," replied Kate as she began to stand.

"And what might your fine father have told ya about believin' everything ya read?"

"He was talking about newspapers not hymnals," Kate placed extra stress on *newspapers*.

"Newspapers and hymnals both doin' their best to spread the word. All I'm sayin' is it's just as easy to hear the other side of the story and consider it for what it might be, Miss Dunn. And givin' the history of your ancestors, I was thinkin' ya might consider the facts as presented. If ya get my gist of the matter?" Flann slowly strummed his fingers in front of his mouth as if he were typing his words on a cloud of pipe smoke.

"Credit is given where credit is due. That's what my father says," responded Kate.

Flann was rescued by Mary Garvey's gurgling, mucus drenched words, which she remedied by giving a firm blow into the remains of an overused tissue. "Why did the Straw Spiders wait so long to cure the nun?"

"I'm goin' to be answering the question the best I can. All I'm about to say is that the deeds of the Straw Spiders are best spoken of and not about." Flann placed a hand on each knee and studied the tile floor, smiling and waiting for Kate Dunn to respond.

"That makes no sense at all," retorted Kate.

"Of and not about Miss Dunn."

2

A PURPLE CREATURE.
LAMPSHADES AND A SECRET.

Kate united with her companion after a hurried hunt in the covers. She was baptized by Kate's tears and showered in her laughter. Together they survived chickenpox, measles, and mumps. She was a shipmate, who sailed with Kate on the Sea of Bad Dreams, where black-hooded ogres clutching yardsticks surfaced from sewer drains and chased them through the streets of Washington Heights.

Melinda was born on Herald Square, in Macy's toy department, plucked from the floor and delivered by baby Katherine, who pulled her from a half-open box as she padded along toward her first Santa visit. Melinda, with her hotdog shape, fit snuggly under Katherine's tiny arm. In place of a nose, Melinda had a trunk, similar to an elephant's. But the stuffed toy wasn't close to being an elephant. She had no floppy ears or eyes that anyone could see. She did not make a sound, lacked moving parts, and was clad in purple fur that resembled the carpet in Mrs. Carlo's living room on the Delicious Fourth Floor.

Liam had attempted to replace Katherine's Melinda with a beautiful doll. A doll whose emerald eyes fluttered and rolled shut when her head tilted back. A queen of a doll with a glistening tiara crowning her head. A doll a father could be proud of, who obediently uttered a word or two when the string on the nape of her neck received a tug. The doll, with its price tag hidden within layers of lace, sat at Mrs. Claus's feet amid a glorious rendition of the North Pole.

Children waiting to warm Santa's lap, watched as Liam worked to coax Melinda from his daughter. He wound up dogs, cats, a fire truck, and a scary witch that looked very much out of place. A silver airplane, with flashing red and green lights and sparks spewing from its propellers led the way and ordained Katherine a reluctant grand marshal. It was a valiant effort by Liam, but Melinda remained attached to baby Katherine's arm while her face morphed into a defiant scowl.

On Christmas morning, Liam watched with dismay as two-year-old Katherine set to work knocking pegs into their proper holes and twisting giant wood screws in place. The workbench was a gift for Rory, but he was more interested in the airplane that had failed, like the doll, to distract his sister. From her second Christmas right up to The Freeze that held Washington Heights in a vice like grip, Kate Dunn pounded every peg into every hole meant to challenge her.

■ ■ ■

Kate was more drowsy than awake. She rubbed her eyes and scanned the area carefully, as when she suspected Danny of snooping about, checking to see whether the spiders she dreamed of had invaded her room. Flann McFarland and his cryptic words-of and not about, had created all of this annoying turbulence churning within her.

A stepstool, more like a miniature ladder, sat in its corner next to an orange crate with jars of paint and pads of paper and an old NYPD shirt transformed into a multicolored smock. Her modeling clay and a giant jar of white paste along with a host of art supplies remained untouched. Her *Encyclopedia Britannica* and the rows of books surrounding her still sat neatly aligned on the pine shelves that her father had installed years ago that hid wallpaper portraits of weeping circus clowns.

Kate rolled a strand of Melinda's fur between her thumb and forefinger. A peaceful ritual that had begun on their first night together.

Melinda's colleagues, a stuffed cat, a squirrel and two brown rabbits found themselves evicted from Kate's bed and lived a life of solitude scattered about her room.

At times, thoughts of exiling Melinda tempted Kate, and Melinda found herself on a shelf whispering in the cat's ear, when Mary spent the night. But always, on the following morning, Kate decided her decision had been premature and Melinda once again shared Kate's pillow.

Kate kicked off her blanket and slid her feet into a pair of reindeer slippers. She crossed her legs, toyed with the drooping antlers on her left foot, and spent a Christmas wish hoping Rory would not replace them. Her big brother's source of income during the winter was shoveling snow. Since Flann's weather forecast of the snow frozen in the clouds remained in effect, Rory's funds were exhausted.

Of all the other pieces of furniture in the room besides her bed, the vanity Liam built was her favorite. Custom-made for Kate, it also served as a desk, as nice as the one Liam had seen his daughter admiring in the window of Stein's discount furniture on 181st Street at one-third the cost. Kate sat on the bench seat that matched the vanity. Dozens of Jack Kennedy campaign buttons fashioned a perimeter around the mirror and framed a collage of Ricky Nelson photographs neatly snipped from *Teen* magazine.

She buried her face in a white towel and inhaled the sterile scent of bleach. Quickly, she spun the towel around her head, creating a nun's habit. Her face turned pink and then cherry red as she tightened the towel and contemplated the name she would take if she made good on her most recent threat to enter the convent.

"Sister Katherine," whispered Kate as she loosened the towel. "Sister Katherine Marie."

Kate's convent threat no longer caught the attention of its intended targets. She made a mental note to add something more menacing to her arsenal for the coming New Year, something more disastrous than a daughter banished and parents deprived of grandchildren.

"Sister Thumbelina. That's what they will call me," muttered Kate. The smallness curse haunted her as Christmas loomed. Gifts of clothing that did not fit would again litter her designated space under the tree just as they had the past two Christmases. Her mother would again perform alterations on the ancient Singer sewing machine, borrowed from Mrs. Stern, who lived on top floor and monitored the comings and goings of anyone who opened the battered steel door that led to the roof.

Kate shook her head free of the temporary habit. Her hair, the color of wheat a week before harvest, collapsed on her shoulders. She picked up her brush and contemplated hairstyles she knew would offend the nuns of Incarnation School and her father. She teased her hair into a frenzy, a style preferred by Monica Broome, who lived on the fifth floor and worked part time at the High Spot Bar as a dinnertime waitress. Monica spent the rest of her week in Brian Kelly's law office as a file clerk, even though Mike Hickey, the full-time bartender at the High Spot, said she would have a hard time alphabetizing past the letter B. Kate tried a ponytail next, a fashion somewhat accepted by the nuns and fully approved of by her father.

Her parents often told her how pretty she was, but she dismissed that as parental obligatory comments. Kate had felt on occasion that her appearance possessed some promising possibilities. Her nose had a slight upward slope, so perfect it could have served as a template for a plastic surgeon. Her ears, neatly tucked away, were almost elflike, but no one would dare use the name of Kate Dunn in the same breath with elf. People found themselves spellbound by her sapphire eyes that snared them into an awkward stare. All agreed that her eyes were a jubilee of blue, like cathedral stained glass that would have mesmerized Tiffany himself.

It was true her features were in flawless proportion, but that was because everything stopped growing in unison, unlike Beatrice Smith, the only girl in eighth grade who was shorter than Kate, by half an inch. Beatrice stood in front of Kate when the nuns ordered them to line up by size. She stopped growing too, but her head never received the message and sat upon her shoulders like a double scoop of ice cream on a sugar cone.

Kate shuffled three steps wrapped in a red robe that had been bulky last year and remained that way. She entered the bathroom and once again became distracted by the cracks in the tile floor and remained convinced that they resembled the face of an old man. She mounted the stool kept under the sink and removed a tube of toothpaste from a medicine cabinet filled with a variety of free sample cold remedies hung on the doorknobs of 650. Samples belonging to tenants who had forgone a Christmas envelope for Flann wound up in a shabby trunk hidden behind the coal chute in the basement.

She moved one of the three tugboats Danny docked next to the toothbrush holder. The remainder of his armada sat moored on the rim of a blizzard - white porcelain bathtub elevated off the floor by four brass ducks.

Kate's father claimed the windowsill as his own. A shaving cup with the image of a faded sailboat, a bottle of after-shave, his communal family gift every Christmas, sat flanked by a shaving brush and a straight razor folded shut.

Toothpaste and saliva accumulated in Kate's mouth puffing her cheeks out like a hamster's. She heard her father beating a dozen eggs. She knew the aroma of bacon would serve as an alarm clock for Rory and Danny. She emptied her mouth and hopped off the stool.

Kate paused in the narrow hallway that connected the five rooms within apartment thirty-one. She knelt down and peeked into the kitchen from just above the floor, a strategy borrowed from a Nancy Drew novel. The kitchen was large by Washington Height's standards. There was room for a Formica topped table and five chairs and after some proper cramming, space for a washing machine connected to the sink that delighted Danny when it loudly shuddered. A yellow four-burner gas stove with an oven big enough to roast a twelve-pound turkey on Christmas morning left enough room for the Dunn family to move about in a well-rehearsed dance.

Liam turned toward the kitchen door, and asked, "How'd we sleep?" Frustrated yet again that she had been detected, Kate retreated and leaned on the hallway wall. It was impossible to encroach upon Liam Dunn. Kate spun around the door and into the kitchen.

"Morning Dad."

Kate had never accepted the mustache Liam had grown last Christmas along with his sideburns after he requested a transferred to the Narcotics

Division. She thought it was a silly attempt to look younger than his forty-eight years and would fool no one.

Liam was as at home in the kitchen as he was on the pistol range. He removed two black iron skillets stored in the oven and began to peel off strips of bacon. "You know what today is don't you?" Liam struck a match and brought two burners to life. They both knew the answer. The game had begun between them when Kate was five.

"It's Monday," replied Kate. It was six days before Christmas.

"I know that." Liam adjusted the gas and carefully laid down each strip of bacon, "I mean, do you know what day it is?" The bacon began its crackling serenade.

"The day after Sunday and the day before Tuesday," said Kate.

"Tree Day is what I'm thinking about. Maybe your brothers might be up for it?"

"Danny has been ready since August," joked Kate.

Liam steered a clump of butter around the smaller skillet and added the eggs urging them to form with a gentle push of a spatula. Alone time with her father was rare. Kate knew it would not last. It never did. Kate knew not to ruin it by sharing her dreams of accomplishing great things it hurt too much. She had once spoken of becoming an attorney. Liam had said nothing and continued reading the paper. She had once spoken of becoming a doctor. Liam agreed with the nuns. "Girls become nurses."

Kate continued to struggle with her father's beer-enhanced words spoken last year at a distant cousin's wedding, "Too bad the brains didn't wind up with my son."

Kate was more than smart, and her academic achievements were a ritual on Awards Day every year starting with first grade and were common knowledge in the halls of 650 and Incarnation School.

"And now the medal for Overall Excellence," a already bored Sister Mary of the Crucifix's, nasal voice filled the auditorium. "Katherine Dunn."

Fathers often spoke with their children about their day. Kate thought that had to be true. Mary's father worked for UPS, and Kate felt confident thinking that Mr. Garvey mentioned a box a customer or the traffic in downtown Brooklyn. Sean O'Leary heard something concerning the trains running in and out of Penn Station where his father worked as a mechanic, Kate was certain of that. There was no doubt in her mind that Joey Carlo's dad returned home with hysterically funny stories about the people who rode in his cab.

Liam Dunn never discussed police matters with Kate, her brothers, or his wife. Just as he never discussed the flesh missing from his lower back that made his swimming trunks hang awkwardly on his right hip. Colleen shared all that she could with Rory and Kate. "Something happened when your father was in the Marines. On an island called Tarawa." After hearing that Kate went to the library on 179th Street and found a history book on the Second World War in the Pacific. She read a chapter and returned the book to its shelf. The pictures of Tarawa dismissed any need to ask questions.

Liam shared less information with the family after the transfer to Narcotics. He spoke only of his hours: when he would be home and when he would not, day tours and night tours, weekends and holidays. The Dunn family understood the drill.

Kate heard little Danny fly past the kitchen door, on his way to study the cracks in the bathroom floor. Last week, he was sure it was a pirate ship. Everything had become about pirates since Kate had taken him to see *Peter Pan* at the palatial Loews Theatre on 173rd Street, where they shared popcorn washed down with cream soda.

Rory trudged into the kitchen clad in his New York Giants football jersey, a second layer of skin that he slept in every night, a walking shrine to his hero, number seventy, Sam Huff. He was a replica of the man preparing breakfast, with the same sharp nose, jutting chin and auburn hair.

His face was in transit, leaving a boyhood depot, destined for manhood, with Liam's Old Spice fertilizing the faint trace of facial hair beginning to sprout.

"Thinking of going for the tree tonight. You guys up for that?" asked Liam. The bacon was ready, seared to a perfect crispness with an aroma that would linger in the kitchen until lunchtime.

"We got a real nice one last year," said Kate.

"Remember when Danny wanted to get that aluminum tree from Woolworths? Imagine. A metal Christmas tree. What would happen if a live wire touched the darn thing?" asked Rory grabbing his plate and half the bacon.

"That tree would have had to be grounded to the radiator, because electricity has to have a path to complete a circuit," explained Kate. "The ground wire would be essential, but I guess you knew that."

Rory looked at their father and shrugged. He had grown accustomed to his sister's off-the-cuff science and history lessons. Kate's parochial school science fair project enhanced her knowledge of electricity. Without surprising anyone, she took first place with her model of a power plant, which still sat in a showcase and welcomed visitors to Incarnation School.

"Any coffee left?" asked Colleen as she removed from the cupboard a green mug inscribed with a white shamrock, proclaiming her, *Number one Mom*.

"Here ya go, my lady." Liam filled her cup from an ancient coffee pot.

Colleen nestled herself under her husband's arm. Being ten inches shorter than him made for a good fit. She wore a white Chinese robe, embroidered with a red dragon, with green eyes and a matching tongue that spewed fire across her back. The robe was a present from Liam on their first Christmas together, when he was a rookie cop working Chinatown.

Colleen was a handsome woman, her skin smooth and opaque like sea glass, possessing its own unique translucency. Her well-defined cheekbones shielded blue eyes that cast an aura of concern, even when she smiled. She kept a youthful promise to Liam, so her ash-blond hair seldom yielded to scissors and flowed down her back without a trace of gray. She was one of the few mothers who worked outside of the home, having taken a job when Danny began first grade. It was part of Colleen and Liam's plan, and it fueled their secret dreams.

Colleen was going to fill out an application at the Lofts Candy store on 183rd Street when she noticed the help wanted sign in the window of Ludlow Lampshades and Upholsterers on the corner of 178th Street and Audubon Avenue. A bronze bell, attached to the door rang halfheartedly when Colleen entered. A fan that appeared perilously loose swayed from a copper ceiling and failed to move August air cemented in humidity. It was a pleasant shop, with a radio permanently tuned to a classical music station that enticed shoppers like a snake charmer. It was so warm and inviting that customers felt they might be in someone's living room. The proprietor of the store, Mrs. Edith Ludlow, the widow of Mr. Ludlow, conducted her life the same way she created lampshades a solid frame with the fabric pulled as taut as possible.

She was a woman who guarded her age as closely as the balance in her checkbook. She avoided giving or receiving hugs, even from her grandchild. Her preference was a handshake and she considered herself blessed with a firm grip.

"May I help you?" asked Mrs. Ludlow stepping from behind a black curtain.

"I was wondering if the job was still available," replied Colleen.

Mrs. Ludlow opened a pack of Parliaments, lit a cigarette with a lighter engraved with her deceased husband's name, exhaled a plume of smoke that hung over her like the thunderheads forming over Washington Heights.

Colleen described the workshop in the rear of the store to Liam that night as "a disorderly organized mess." Fabric was everywhere, spooled and stacked like cords of wood and heaped on metal shelves that almost touched the ceiling. Scattered about were hundreds of sample books loaded with swatches of cloth of every texture and color. A three-cushion sofa and two armchairs stripped down to their frames sat on the shop floor where a black man, tall enough to make everything around him shrink plied his craft. He glanced in Colleen's direction and extended a polite nod and matching smile.

Colleen took the job and she worked from eight to three-thirty-five days a week with an occasional Saturday morning if things at the shop got busy, which they began to do. Her hours allowed her to be home when Danny and Kate arrived from school and she greeted them with a cup of hot chocolate in the winter and iced tea in the summer. Mrs. Ludlow tutored Colleen on how to miserly measure fabric and sew tight seams. She became deadly accurate with a small tack hammer, a fact that fascinated Liam whenever he visited the shop with Danny.

"Dad says we are going for the tree tonight," said Kate. Liam handed her a plate with three slices of bacon and a share of the eggs as she took her assigned seat at the table next to Rory. The sound of Danny and his glider Dart filled the air. The roar that came from the throat of a six-year-old stunned people. As soon as he entered the kitchen, Liam swept him up in his arms and placed him on the washing machine.

"How's New York's best pilot this morning?" Liam asked as he prepared a Superman plate with two slices of bacon and a small portion of eggs that he hoped Danny would eat.

"Test pilot. Kate says I am a test pilot. Right Kate?"

"That's right." Kate paused from eating and smiled gently at Danny. She looked down at her plate knowing if she expressed an interest in flying, her father would tell her to become a stewardess.

"I'm going to test fly Dart out the window," said Danny, full of confidence.

"That would be cool," Rory quickly added.

"No, it wouldn't Rory! We fly that plane in the park," snapped Kate.

"Calm down, Kate. Maybe the rest of us don't live our lives waiting for catastrophe to strike," said Rory, totally annoyed.

"Don't listen to Rory. You stay away from the windows Danny," Kate's fork took the form of a weapon pointed at her little brother, "or I promise no more trips to the park for you or Dart."

"Katherine's right Danny, you know the window rule," said Colleen.

Danny crossed his legs Indian style and settled in atop the washing machine where he picked through his meals. Eating there added a smidgen more of space around the table.

Liam enjoyed telling the cops he worked with that his Danny had, "two speeds: full blast and off."

It appeared nature was undecided as to how Danny Dunn would look on his tenth birthday, more like his sister or his brother. At age six his parents' genes were at work with Liam contributing his auburn hair and Colleen her cheekbones and blue eyes.

"Hey, Danny, guess what?" said Rory, changing the subject as he maneuvered one last morsel of breakfast onto his fork.

"What? What do I have to guess?" asked Danny pushing his eggs around Superman's cape with a rigid slice of bacon.

"No guessing Danny. We're going for our tree. And I have a feeling it will be just as big as last year's," said Rory.

"Kate, do you think the Straw Spiders will come and visit our tree?" asked Danny.

Kate would be turning thirteen, past the age of believing in Santa Claus and the Easter Bunny, but she played along like her family for Danny's sake, stacking cookies and filling a glass with milk on Christmas Eve. And it was Kate's "magic key" that opened all doors that kept Santa alive when Danny worried the Gracie Mansion yule log on channel eleven was not a suitable fireplace for Santa to use to make his annual entrance.

"I have no idea," said Kate barely above a whisper.

"No idea? That's a first," announced Rory.

Kate gritted her teeth, a warning like a rattle snake before it strikes and looked up at Rory. He towered above his sister even when they were sitting. Height was the only advantage Rory had over his sister. But Kate was not in the mood for a one-sided shouting match. When Kate verbally arm-wrestled with Rory, he found himself pinned before the contest started.

"I would like them to come. I would like to see the Straw Spiders," said Danny enthusiastically.

"Fat chance of that, Danny, because it has to snow while the Christmas trees are up," explained Rory.

"That's not fair. Flann said the snow is frozen in the clouds," complained Danny.

"He's still doing weather forecasts?" Colleen sounded surprised.

"Oh yes," said Kate coming back to life, "still in control of the weather."

Rory climbed up on his chair. "As an alumnus of the Flann McFarland after-school Hallway University I can assure you no one has ever seen a Straw Spider."

"No one?" Danny did not take the news well.

Liam stepped back from Danny's view and waved his spatula, a signal to Rory, letting him know to back off. When Rory was Danny's age, he was a big Straw Spider fan, almost equaling his feelings for Sam Huff. Rory stepped off the chair. "Well ah … no one yet, anyways, I am sure someday somebody will. Flann said it has to snow when the trees are up, and it hasn't since I have been around. So, I have never seen a Straw Spider. That's all I'm trying to say, Danny."

"Flann says we're not allowed to talk about them. Right, Kate?" Danny said respectfully.

"Right, we can only talk *of* them and not *about* them; that's part of the legend."

"I know what we can talk about," said Liam. "We can talk about you guys cleaning up this kitchen."

Liam and Colleen let their children perform their assigned chores. Rory set to work at the sink scouring the skillets with steel wool while Kate scraped off the dishes. Danny remained safely perched within his nest on the washing machine, keeping a safe distance from the window.

■ ■ ■

Liam closed the French doors that separated their bedroom from the living room. He could hear the sound raise on the radio. Rory had changed the station to WMCA without any protest from Kate and The Kingston Trio sang and asked, "Where Have All the Flowers Gone," and the laughter of the Dunn children filled apartment thirty-one.

It never mattered if the sun was rising or setting in Washington Heights. The Dunn bedroom would remain cloaked in a shadow, trapped in the alley formed by the six-story garage next to 650. Liam and Colleen attempted to brighten the space by hanging wallpaper depicting a Greek temple with goddesses pouring water from elaborate ewers. Their efforts became a private joke between husband and wife sparing the Greeks from a trip on the dumbwaiter.

Two small potted plants on either side of the French doors had died within a week and now resided on the fire escape, where a dish of birdseed fed a band of frolicking sparrows who arrived at dawn and vanished at dusk. A coat of antique white applied to three walls by the landlord's painters created a permanent cloudy day. Their shared dresser filled a corner and served as a shelf for their wedding portrait with Liam standing tall in Marine dress blues, his chest home to a Purple Heart and Navy Cross, and Colleen, captured in her youth, clad in a no-frills wedding dress, the same dress worn by her mother, her something borrowed.

Colleen withdrew to a double bed flanked by two matching night tables, holding lamps with shades created during her lunch hour. Liam turned to Colleen. The Chinese robe caught his attention. Liam silently wished their kids were in school. It was time for their secret, a special secret, best kept and shared with someone close to the heart. There was no one who had ever been closer to Liam's heart than his wife.

Colleen's eyelids let down their guard, allowing a restful calm to caress her face. She removed a manila envelope from under the mattress and held it in her lap. Liam joined Colleen on their bed, placed his arm around her shoulder, and kissed her forehead.

3

FLANN'S MUSEUM AND A TROUBLESOME FAUCET.

Flann's impotent arms, ripened by old age into Jell-O, struggled to steady a half shovel of coal. His labored breaths sounded like a fluttering engine about to stall when he shoved the furnace door shut, sealing the mouth of the iron beast. He cranked open valves attached to a dozen rusted conduits, aortas carrying heat from the belly of 650 through steam pipes and radiators. Within minutes, black smoke, laden with toxic soot spewed from the smokestack, releasing a stench over Washington Heights.

Ten years earlier Flann had purchased a uniform. He thought it appropriate for a man who held the title of building superintendent. When the tenants ventured to the cellar, they found Flann clad in a pair of khaki pants and matching shirt. Ending just above his ankles were a pair of brown boots he kept neatly buffed but never polished. Kate compared the brass ring hanging from his belt to a hula-hoop that held hundreds of keys, many of which opened locks that no longer existed but added to Flann's air of authority. The jangling sound of the keys trailed Flann as he hobbled toward the two rooms that were his home, a cramped concealed cove, between the boiler room and storage room, where stowed away were bikes, sleds, carriages, and steamer trunks filled with family treasures. Hanging twenty-watt light bulbs, all the Lord of the Land Mr. Crumble allowed, hung from mildewed ceilings, and cast a dreary half-light on dank brick walls.

Flann was the curator of 650's discarded art. Crashing waves hung on his cellar walls adjacent to faded street scenes of Paris and Rome. Leaping ballerinas performed for paint-by-number images of cats and dogs created by aspiring artists on rainy summer days, when the clouds above Washington Heights drank of the Hudson River and then drenched the streets, sending stickball players scurrying for hallways.

Flann managed the pain in his left hip by keeping himself akin to a ship with a twenty-degree list to the port side. He paused at weigh points in the cellar allowing the pain to subside and light his pipe. His favorite safe harbor was beneath Van Gogh's *The Starry Night*. The print had been left behind by a tenant who vanished after Flann posted the third late rent notice on his door. He would study the masterpiece through clouds of Cherry Blend and wondered why Vincent opted not to share his canvas with at least one constellation.

A jubilant Christmas vision greeted Flann. Mr. Hooper, from apartment thirty-three, a magi in Flann's mind, was about to slip a green envelope under his door. Flann decorated the door the day after Thanksgiving with three hundred twinkling green and red lights, a beacon that reminded the tenants, believers, and non-believers that Christmas was approaching: Christmas, the season for casting aside frivolous differences, allowing all to partake in the joy of giving.

"And a fine day to you Mr. Hooper. And how might your lovely bride Mrs. Hooper be? 'tis a lucky man you are, sir. Lucky indeed." Flann's back became as straight as a West Point cadet's. He did his best not to stare at the envelope.

"She'd be happier if you replaced that faucet," said Hooper.

Hooper never left his apartment without a tie around his neck or a pen in his shirt pocket. A fit sixty-year-old who kept his social conversations to a few well-placed words, his controlled irritability allowed him to sell insurance. "The faucet you were going to fix in July," said Hooper as nicely as he could.

"And wasn't it just yesterday I was on the phone with our landlord Mr. Crumble. And wasn't it about your very unfortunate situation?"

"When are you going to fix it Flann?"

"And what if I were to tell ya that annoying drip will be gone, out of your life before Christmas? What might ya be thinkin' about that?" asked Flann.

Flann had Hooper wondering. Was he talking about the faucet or the Lord of the Land?

"Of what year?" said Hopper, a tad testy.

"Why this very year. And what if I told ya this very week? And what if I told ya tomorrow?!"

"Are you telling me tomorrow?" said Hooper pessimistically. It frustrated him that every spoken sentence was a question when a simple answer was all he required.

"And why would I not?"

"Well I'll be holding you to that Flann. And I mean it," said Hooper waving the envelope in the air. Flann could not help but notice that it appeared a mite thicker than last year. *More people must be betting they are going to die*, thought Flann, thankful that Mr. Hooper shared the bounty.

"Here you are Flann. Merry Christmas," said Hooper handing over the envelope.

"And a very Merry Christmas to you. And a fine and happy New Year as well," said Flann with a polite bow.

Hooper trekked up the cellar steps battling The Freeze with every step and feeling that he had just purchased a new faucet.

4

SHADOWS, PISTOLS, AND TREES.

Kate tapped twice on the steam pipe in her room. The two friends used what Kate called the SPCS, the Steam Pipe Communication System, for last-minute events that dictated an immediate response. Mary quickly returned three raps from her room two floors above Kate.

Kate opened her window and poked her head over a window guard she had decorated with blue lights. The Freeze stung her ears and vaporized her words in a frozen cloud.

"Mary, see if your mom will let you go with us to get our tree!"

Mary gave a firm blow into a tissue, causing Kate to roll her eyes.

"Okay, wait a minute." Mary disappeared and returned as quickly as if she had never left, "She says okay, but have to be back by eight."

Danny scurried down the stairs with Dart firmly in his hand. A Davy Crockett coonskin hat sheltered his head, its bushy tail swinging like a clocks pendulum across his back. He applied his brakes in front of apartment twenty-one. After a hasty look at the barren door, he dashed down the stairs like a startled squirrel.

Mary watched Flann replace two burned out Christmas bulbs on the front door of 650. Her arsenal of tissues stood ready and protruded from her coat pockets. She wore a knitted hat, which Kate thought looked rather silly with a snowball above each ear that concealed her red hair.

Flann created a proper festive atmosphere in the small vestibule by hanging strings of blinking Christmas lights around the ceiling that reflected on the mailboxes he shined to a glass like luster during the of month of December. He acted bowled over when Danny jumped down the last two steps, landing with a thump, his raccoon hat sliding onto his nose.

"And let me catch my breath. 'Tis that Donald Crockett himself!" exclaimed Flann pointing his pipe at Danny.

"Davy, Flann. Davy Crockett," said Danny quickly correcting Flann.

"Right. Donald 'tis that dog."

"Pluto is the dog. Donald is the duck!"

Danny loved the bantering that occurred when he discovered Flann working in the halls of 650.

"And how could I keep forgetin'? A good thing, Danny, I'm havin' ya to be remindin' me."

The Dunn family resembled a group of Artic explorers outfitted to confront The Freeze. Kate understood her father's wardrobe included his gun. The weapon went everywhere they went and set Liam apart from other fathers. The gun impressed Kate and Rory's friends and Danny's playmates.

Kate knew it was as an equalizer, a tool her father needed to protect himself from criminals who carried guns.

The weapon created a whirlpool of fear that devoured her when the sound of sirens ricocheted throughout Washington Heights. Kate was ten when Liam summoned her to the kitchen, as Rory had been, as Danny would be. As matter-of-factly, as a father pouring a glass of milk for his child Liam removed his service revolver from the locked cabinet over the refrigerator and sat next to Kate. The scent of gun oil mingled with a brewing pot of coffee. He placed the unloaded black pistol in front of her. Liam understood his Kate was curious about everything, including the gun. He also understood that this inquisitiveness could lead to death. Confronted by the pistol sitting in stark contrast to the white tablecloth, Kate lost interest.

"Pick up the weapon, Kate," said Liam.

"I don't need to," Kate said, staring at the weapon.

"It's important for me to know that you have handled this weapon, Kate. You will hold it and examine it," he ordered, "and you will aim it at the wall over the sink, and you will never touch the weapon again."

Liam gently lifted his daughter's face by placing a finger under her chin. "Do you fully understand what I am asking of you?"

Kate picked up the pistol and slowly turned it. Its weight astonished her. She needed both hands to steady it. She pointed the barrel at the wall over the sink. Within seconds, the weapon began to weave up and down and then left to right, as if it possessed a life of its own. She placed it back on the table vowing silently to never touch it again. "I understand," said Kate.

"And where might you be off to if you're not mindin' my askin', Danny?" asked Flann.

"It's Tree Day, Flann," said Danny enthusiastically.

"As fine a crop as I have ever seen are planted all over Washington Heights," said Flann.

"Is the snow still frozen in the clouds, Flann? I want it to snow for Christmas," said Danny.

"I'm afraid to be sayin' right now 'tis looking that way Danny," said Flann lighting his pipe.

"Believe it will snow, Danny, and it will," said Grimes from apartment twenty-one in her tiny voice that caused people to pay close attention.

"Really? Oh, boy Flann, did you hear that? Here come the Straw Spiders," proclaimed Danny.

"Now, Danny, don't be getting yourself all worked up about something that's not goin' to be happening," said Flann puffing on his pipe, sending a cloud of Cherry Blend to the ceiling, fogging in the Christmas lights.

The Dunn family stepped aside to let the Grimes woman past. She stopped and smiled into little Danny's face, an easy task since Danny was an inch taller than her. Her eyes were hidden behind the carnival glasses even though the sun had set. The only change in her appearance was a small silver Christmas angel attached to her black turban.

"I'm afraid I'll have to be disagreeing with ya Miss Grimes. Or might it be Mrs. Grimes?" asked Flann puffing on his pipe and doing his best to hide a smirk.

Grimes turned toward Flann and tilted her head quickly like a bird toward the ceiling and then straightened it, the way she did on the street. She stepped forward to where Flann stood and looked straight up as if he were the Chrysler Building.

"Miss Grimes. Miss H. Wellington Grimes," replied Grimes seriously.

"I'm sorry to have to tell ya that in addition to the fact that it will not be snowing there is no way I can fit 'Miss H. Wellington Grimes' on a mailbox. It will have to remain as 'tis. That would be Grimes. The way Mr. Crumble himself presented it to me. Of course, I could be putin' ya in the mailbox if ya would prefer that."

"That's not funny, Flann!" said Kate.

"Yes, it is," contradicted Rory.

"You stay out of it, Rory. You got a pass yesterday, don't push your luck!"

"That's okay Kate," interceded Grimes, "mail arrives just as quickly for Grimes as it does for H. Wellington Grimes."

Kate sensed that an unwelcome visitor had trespassed into Flann's Shiloh.

"Is that Flann with one N or two?" said Grimes, toying with Flann.

"It would be two Miss Grimes," replied Flann with a chuckle.

"I have two n's in my name too Miss H. Grimes," said Danny.

"H. Wellington Grimes Danny," said Rory loudly.

"Now that the spelling bee is over, we will be on our way," interrupted Liam, opening the door for his family. Liam paused and leaned into Flann's hearin' ear, "Well, be interesting to see those Straw Spiders you've been talking about if Grimes is right."

"I never spoke about them sir. Only of them," said Flann.

■ ■ ■

The tree shoppers coasted down the steps of 650. The air stung the skin that they dared to expose like the crack of a whip and reminded them that their coat was their best friend. The Freeze became a schoolyard bully finally confronted.

The citizens of Washington Heights had decided to go about their business. Instead of staying in, people were going out. Kate reminded anyone who would listen how awful it must have been for the shoeless Continental Army encamped just a few blocks away at Fort Tryon Park in the winter of 1778.

Danny and Rory scampered toward Broadway past ancient brown lampposts. Swans of cast iron with bent necks clutching glass globes emitting amber halos. Danny stopped running and launched Dart. A breeze snatched the plane and lifted it into the night sky. It circled a lamppost and then orbited manhole covers that served as bases during summer stickball games, played until darkness prevailed over the streets of Washington Heights.

The plane completed a second shorter loop as the frigid wind faded and returned to Danny, as if an invisible string spun from silk connected it to him. Liam had been watching Dart's flight as he watched all that went on.

Liam's seniority allowed him to claim Christmas week his vacation. Once he left 650, the vacation became secondary. His eyes scanned 177th Street like a sweeping radar screen. Familiar faces gave a nod, thankful a cop made their street his personal beat.

A body moved within the shallow, dark doorway of Tip Top Printing. The shop was next to an alley and a favorite attraction in the summer, drawing hordes of young spectators taking a break from endless summer games of street skully, hide-and-seek and ringolevio. A perfumed wave of chemicals washed over the sidewalk when Mr. Garfunkel opened his door to vent the heat. Kate watched, fascinated by the three printing presses that huffed and puffed compressed air pushing paper over inked rollers.

Liam's eyes locked on the doorway. The figure slowly emerged and turned east in the direction of Wadsworth Avenue. Liam took mental notes:

> Height: Five feet seven inches.
> Weight: 140 to 150 pounds.
> Hat: Blue. Wool. Watch cap.
> Jacket: Pea Coat style.

■ ■ ■

Wherever Danny glanced, Christmas stared back. There was no contain-
ing the excitement percolating within him, and so, without any warning or
giving a hoot as to what anyone might think, he danced around the street,
performing his own choreographed steps, hopping on one foot and then
the other in a circle and then zigzagging past smiling pedestrians.

Liam caught up with his son, and after a short chase he tossed Danny
on to his shoulders, placing him closer to the glorious giant stars that
spanned Broadway creating a bridge of light that shone as radiantly as
the twinkle in every child's eye. A electrical storm of Christmas light that
glowed over the sidewalks and sutured shadows on to the heels of the citizens of Washington Heights.

Kate clung to Mary's arm as tightly as Colleen clung to Liam enjoying the
festive sight that everyone yearned for all year. Store windows were decorated
in competition with their neighbor. Some had mangers and others a small tree
or a Dickens' village. Glass doors and giant windows were smothered in a blizzard of canned snow and etched with stenciled Santa faces and amusing elves.
Droves of passersby carried presents and towed happy children who looked
up at Danny struggling to keep the raccoon hat out of his eyes.

The tree-shopping caravan huddled together in front of Hobby Land.
They meshed with scores of children gazing in astonishment at a colos-
sal mechanical spaceman who gave a friendly mechanical wave to all, as a
black Lionel locomotive miraculously puffed smoke and hauled a freight
train of Christmas dreams around his legs.

"Oh, wow Mary," Kate spoke barely above a whisper into Mary's
wool-covered ear.

"What?" asked Mary while wiping her nose.

Kate nodded toward a secret Christmas wish. A wish needing no alterations, a wish that did not rely on Dunn genes to provide her with
those yearned for two inches in height. High in the corner, adjacent to
a gargantuan panda bear was a telescope, a snow-white tube on a tripod
trimmed in black. Kate would never ask for such a gift; it was far too
extravagant. Her five allotted Christmas presents never totaled the sixty
dollars the telescope cost. Kate loved being on the roof in the summer

with her stars and President Kennedy's words replaying in her head, challenging America, and daring his compatriots to place a man on the moon and return him safely, not because it was easy but because it was hard.

Kate could locate constellations and was a member of the Hayden Planetarium's astronomers club. She knew the precise moment that Sputnik, the dreaded soviet satellite would invade the sky over Washington Heights. When she observed the green star like sphere, she fretted over what the Russians would launch next.

"Come on Kate!" Danny tugged on his sister's arm pulling her back to Earth.

Danny led the way, half-skipping and running toward 181st Street, where racks of Christmas trees stood at attention in front of storefronts like rigid toy soldiers, pulled from the ranks and presented to families for inspection. If they passed, which most did, they transformed into The Tree for their Christmas.

■ ■ ■

The sign on the streetlamp read 181st street and Saint Nicholas Avenue, but it was Pedro's Corner and everyone called it Pedro's Corner. He worked at his newsstand three hundred and sixty – five-days a year, like the workers who created his papers and the truck drivers who delivered them. A constant stream of commuters trekking toward the subway grabbed his papers and flipped coins in the air that Pedro caught with fingers blackened by a pallet of newspaper ink from the nine daily city papers he sold.

"Here you are. For you, Senor Liam. I been savin' this one for you. What do you think?" Pedro smacked the tree's stump on the sidewalk and pulled down frozen branches.

"It's a beautiful tree Pedro. It really is," said Colleen while admiring the tree.

"It is. But the one at Benny's candy store was nice too." Kate looked at her father, knowing she had scored a point in the important tree negotiation. She was happy for the quick wink sent by Liam.

"Never buy one of dem', not from Benny," interrupted Pedro, "You had better never do that. I am only telling you because I like the Dunn family. Ask Mr. Gurtner, he bought one last year and his cat died."

"Because of the tree?" Colleen asked taken somewhat aback.

"That's what the cat doctor said. The tree had some kind of bugs in it so you better be careful."

Pedro ran the sleeve of his faded army field jacket under his nose. The same jacket he had worn during the Battle of the Bulge in 1945. "Had this tree sold three times for four bucks. That's twelve dollars in my hand but I saved it for my amigo Liam Dunn."

"Hey Pedro, I don't think you can count money you never got," said Rory.

"Let me tell you something Mister Rory young blood. Any time someone offers Pedro money it counts!"

"I don't know Pedro." Liam looked impatiently at his watch, "Four bucks is a little steep."

Pedro shuffled his feet, as if he were dancing with The Freeze. "I'll let you have it for three - fifty. Any less and I might as well give the tree away."

"In two days, you would take three for it," said Liam.

"This one? This tree?" Pedro did his best to act baffled.

"Yeah this tree."

"Are you kidding me around Liam Dunn?"

"No I'm not."

"It won't be here in two days. There's a waitin' list for this tree."

"A waiting list?" Liam laughed.

"Look at this tree pronto Senor Liam Dunn it might be gone in two minutes!"

Kate and her father knew there were no waiting lists or dead cats but it added to the fun of doing business with Pedro.

"Heck, since you bought your tree from Pedro last year, I'm gonna' let you pay three bucks."

Liam looked toward Colleen who smiled with approval, and so Liam conducted the required tree poll.

"Danny?"

"The Straw Spiders will really like this one!" Danny exclaimed.

"Kate?"

"I vote yes."

"Rory?"

"Great tree Dad."

"How about you Mary?"

"Wonderful tree Mr. Dunn," said Mary into a tissue.

Rory completed the trip to 177ᵗʰ street, proud that he did not pass the six-foot tree to his father to carry, impressing the Dunn family and adding another virtue that Mary Garvey could secretly worship in her best friend's brother. They walked once more beneath the friendly lampposts of 177ᵗʰ Street that illuminated their passage home. Liam surveyed the doorway to Tip Top Printing and added to his mental notes that the Stranger was nowhere in sight.

Tree Day had sapped the energy from little Danny Dunn and made another step impossible. He gazed up at his father who lifted him in his arms. Liam slowly followed behind his family, watching Rory, who struggled under the weight of The Tree, totally consumed by his determination to complete the last leg of their trip.

The vision of a marine appeared before Liam, running with a wounded buddy over his shoulder, stepping over the dead and the wounded blotting out Liam's view of Rory. Liam fought with the image, pushing it back away from his family away from 177ᵗʰ Street, back into a dark chamber within his mind, the key to which he alone held.

Colleen and the girls came to an abrupt halt on the second step of 650's stoop. When Rory reached them, he dropped The Tree. Standing in the vestibule, under Flann's Christmas lights, were Nora Downey and her daughter Shannon, holding a shopping bag.

5

LEARN TO DRAW, AND PEOPLE, NOT PLACES.

"Right out to the fire escape Rory and don't knock the bird seed dish off!" Colleen held the door open and stepped aside as Rory charged past with The Tree on his shoulder. Mary stood in awe, astounded by Rory's physical attributes.

"I know Mom. It's like only my fifteenth tree," said Rory.

"Maybe you could help with our tree, Rory," suggested Mary as she climbed the stairs to her apartment.

"Forget it Mary, he only delivers to apartment thirty-one," bemoaned Kate.

Liam clutched a sleeping Danny in his arms and entered the room the brothers shared. He laid Danny gently down and removed the first layer of clothes that insulated him. No room existed in Washington Heights that compared to the Dunn boys. It was a adventurous room, home to a fleet of ships moored on shelves built by Liam. Model fighter planes and bombers circled the ceiling, held aloft by barely visible fishing line. A wooden bi - wing airplane with Snoopy at the controls orchestrated the entire air show. The wooden desk, cluttered with text books and also built by Liam, was larger than Kate's vanity by eight inches in every direction. Taped on the walls were pictures of New York Giants football players that spilled over from a corkboard and surrounded Sam Huff, who stood flanked by Rosey Grier, Andy Robustelli, Frank Gifford, and Y.A. Tittle.

"I should have called, Colleen, I'm sorry," said Nora, removing a worthless coat she would not let her brother Liam replace.

"Don't worry about it." Colleen presumed the phone had once again been turned off. "Katherine take Shannon and get her set up in your room."

"My room?" A stern look from Colleen and Kate was on her way with Shannon and her shopping bag.

"So, when did the boiler go down?" Colleen asked.

"Last night. They thought they could fix it but then there was something about parts. Who knows? The thing has been on the fritz for years."

"Danny is out for the count," said Liam, entering the kitchen. He removed his service revolver and locked it in the cabinet. Liam did not want to ask but he had to. Their parents were dead, Nora was his kid sister and had no one else.

"Where's Ernie?"

"He's working," replied Nora.

Nora had forgotten how to smile. The constant stress of life with an out- of- control drunk fed a river of tears that had forged gullies on her once-pretty face. The working story was a cover not a lie. In cop world, there was a difference. A cover was an attempt to protect a third party. A lie was a thought-out plan to deceive. Liam knew there was no point in asking questions that led to cover answers.

"I'm going to be on my way back," announced Nora.

"You're not going anywhere," said Liam in a cop voice that the Dunn family had learned to endure.

"It's okay. I can turn on the oven Liam, I just wanted to get Shannon out of the cold."

"Do you think I'm going to let you take the subway back to Brooklyn tonight?"

"I guess not." Nora knew that to argue with her brother would be futile.

"Well, you guessed right. We'll talk about it tomorrow," said Liam, giving Nora a hug.

He hoped that the worst-case scenario had not finally played out, leaving his sister and niece out on the street.

"It's okay, Liam. It's the boiler," said Nora.

"Right the boiler," muttered Liam.

■ ■ ■

Shannon's coat was three sizes too small, and when she tried to remove it, it became a strait jacket that trapped her like a dolphin in a commercial fishing net. It appeared as if she would never escape it because it held her in a painful hammerlock, knotting her arms in both sleeves behind her back. Before Kate could execute a rescue, a burst of inner energy ignited within Shannon and she fought free of the garment.

Kate watched as Shannon carefully removed each item from her bag, as if she had just returned from a shopping spree on Fifth Avenue where she had purchased a new wardrobe from fashionable boutiques. The few frayed blouses and a pair of jeans were in stark contrast to the Bloomindales shopping bag, adding to the cruel plight of a child trapped in her parents' poverty. Hard times wrote Shannon Downey her script, but she refused to recite her lines.

There was a subtle likeness between the girls that someone might notice, but only after, he or she learned of their relationship. Kate was two years older and taller by half of an inch, but she knew that would not last another three months. Their hair was the same color, but Shannon's held on to a stubborn natural curl that framed her face.

"You have a nice room," she said.

"Thanks."

"Nice and warm," said Shannon knowingly.

"Yeah, our super, Flann, keeps the hot air blowing, that's for sure. Too bad about your boiler. How long do you think it will be broken?" asked Kate.

"What you mean is, how long do I think I'll be stuck in your room?" replied Shannon coolly.

"That's not what I meant."

"Yes, it is." Shannon folded a T- shirt that featured a washed-out French Poodle that was missing one rhinestone eye and placed it on the bed. "I could see the look on your face when Aunt Colleen told you to take me to your room."

Kate hid her surprise that her cousin was so perceptive; she thought of herself as the master of the no show face she practiced in the mirror, envisioning vile events, and reacting stoically. A life of waiting for the shoe to drop that is what Mary called it.

Kate thought of it as anticipating the arrival of the police commissioner and a priest at the door of apartment thirty-one.

Shannon eyed Melinda, who sat propped up in the corner of the bed. Kate quickly reacted and dropped one of the rabbits on to Shannon's lap. Within a minute, Shannon's attention wandered toward the orange crate box, her eyes fixed on Kate's Jon Gnagy learn to draw pad. A book of still life art lessons sat beneath it.

"You watch John Gnagy? It's on nine o'clock Saturday's channel five. Right before Sky King." It was a stupid question. Kate knew that as soon as she asked it.

Shannon tossed the rabbit across the room. It landed on a shelf that held a tattered copy of *Black's Law Dictionary*. Kate found it on top of the garbage pail outside Brian Kelly's law office. She was up to letter E. *Ex parte: represented by one side.*

"Not anymore. We don't have a TV. Ernie took it to the repair shop. Never came back."

Shannon continued without a hint of remorse, "The toaster my mom got with plaid stamps? That went with Ernie to the repair shop last week."

"Ernie. You mean your father?"

"I mean Ernie. That is what I call him when he's drinking. When he's not drinking I call him Dad but Dad has been Ernie since Thanksgiving."

Kate got up from her vanity and pulled the orange crate box from its corner. "I'm sorry that you have . . ." said Kate sliding the box toward Shannon.

"Don't be," her cousin, said quickly. "Father Horan says there is nothing for anyone to be sorry about. Not me, not my mother, and not you, because we didn't do anything wrong.

The worst thing about being around Ernie is everybody is always sorry about something. Most of all Ernie."

Shannon looked down into the orange crate box. It was a perfect chance for Kate to change the subject away from Ernie – Dad.

"I don't watch his show anymore, he makes me nuts. 'Take your number three pencil then take the number thirty-four pencil then take your blending brush.' He's done with the whole picture by the time I find the stupid brush."

"You have the pencils?" asked Shannon, taken aback.

"Go ahead, it's okay Shannon." Kate pushed the orange crate box closer.

"I draw with a number two pencil. You know . . . a regular number two."

Shannon removed the cop shirt smock exposing the TV artist's numbered pencils that Kate kept sharpened to a fine point. Shannon had never seen some of the colors. She held the number three pencil, Pacific Blue. She carefully replaced it and removed number sixteen, Horse Saddle Brown. She held it up and examined the point of the pencil like a scientist examining a test tube. She opened the pad and felt the texture of the paper, instantly sensing that it was much better than the paper she smuggled home from school. The paper had an almost a cloth like feel and a hue of its own, a faint yellow that took color well.

"Here, take the book. You can copy the pictures. Start with lesson one," instructed Kate.

"I don't like to copy pictures. I draw things from my head."

"Okay, then draw whatever you like."

"I'll draw whatever comes to my head. Even if I don't like it."

■ ■ ■

The rain was falling on the deserted streets of Washington Heights the night Decker arrived to work on the phone. Joe Decker was an engineer for Bell Telephone who told Kate such amazing stories that she thought he possessed a crystal ball where his brain ought to have been.

Before he moved his wife and infant son from apartment ten to Hicksville a year ago, he put a twelve-foot extension cord on the Dunn phone as Liam requested. It allowed him to take the phone from the table by his chair in the living room into the bedroom, safe behind the French doors where he discussed police matters that only the Greek gods pasted on the wall could hear.

"One day, Kate," Decker said looking inside his toolbox, "you are going to call a person and not a place."

"Really Mr. Decker?" Decker inspired Kate with what he had to say. He spoke in a way that made the unbelievable events he predicted seem ten minutes away.

Decker removed a screwdriver from his toolbox. "It's true, Kate. Your world is going to change. Soon you will not be using a rotary phone. Phones will have push buttons that light up when you touch them."

"I would love to have a phone like that."

"You will, and it will be soon, I'd say within two years."

"Amazing! And a person not a place. Do not tell me like Maxwell Smart talking into his shoe on *Get Smart*."

"Just like that but without the shoe of course," said Decker in his usual serious way.

"Of course," said Kate amused by the idea.

"They will be big at first. But as time goes by-I am thinking small enough to fit in a car's glove compartment. The transistor and Telstar have created a new world, Kate. The phone technology is right around the corner. And one day you will own a computer."

"Never," said Kate, taken aback at the thought.

"Yep. You'll see. And you keep working hard, Kate. The future belongs to you."

"Thank you Mr. Decker."

"For what?"

"Including me in the future."

■ ■ ■

Liam closed the bedroom door. He tucked the phone under his chin and flipped open the Zippo lighter that survived the war with him and lit a Lucky Strike. The cigarette smoke irritated his eyes as he dialed the phone while peering through the curtains.

"Manhattan South, Cassidy."

"Liam Dunn."

"Yeah, Merry Christmas Dunn."

"I need a favor."

"Everybody needs a favor."

"Need you to call the five two in Brooklyn."

"I know the five two is in Brooklyn."

"I know you know. I know that."

"Guess I could help you out."

"You're all heart."

"My ex-wife use to say that. Drove me nuts."

"Need to have them send a car over to 328 Chauncey Street. Lean on the super. Gleason is his name and find out if the heat is on."

"Who are you, Dunn? The health department?"

"Right that's me. And I need to know if apartment six is vacant. Can you do that?"

"Merry Christmas."

"Call me. Wadsworth eight – three-eight-four-two."

"I have that."

"Okay. Tonight?"

"Tonight."

6

THE SECRET ENVELOPE AND THE BUCKINGHAM WITCH.

Nora stood in front of the bathroom mirror, raking her nicotine-stained fingers through a forest of matted hair the color of pencil twenty-three, Slate Gray, which enhanced her self-imposed unkempt look. A glimpse at the cracked bathroom tiles fetched her the image of a clown.

The aroma of bacon and the French toast Liam served drenched in maple syrup greeted Nora when she plodded into the kitchen. Like an overwhelmed coach, she delivered a useless pat on her daughter's shoulder. Shannon devoured four thick slices of the battered bread and snatched the last piece of bacon before Rory realized what had happened, making him feel as if he had missed a tackle.

Colleen scampered into the kitchen looking crisp in a black skirt and a red cardigan sweater. Her hair, as always, was neat and functional, parted in the middle and pulled straight back concealing her ears and tightly braided. Under her arm was the envelope from under the mattress.

"Morning Aunt Nora morning Mom," said Kate as she dipped the bread in syrup and moved it about in a preordained pattern, wondering why her mother appeared smartly attired and not clad in slacks, her usual Ludlow shop attire.

"Do you have to go to work Mom? It's Christmas," asked Danny from atop his usual perch, the washing machine, licking the maple syrup off his Superman dish as if it were a giant five-cent lollypop.

"It's not Christmas yet Danny and yes I have to get to work."

Nora fumbled with a skillet in the sink, attempting the impossible, trying to be useful in another woman's kitchen. "Thanks for helping us out," she said, drying her hands with Colleen's Santa Claus towel.

"Everywhere you look, you see boiler repair trucks. I'm afraid the whole city is breaking down.

Who knows, our boiler could go any minute," said an upbeat Colleen.

"Where are we going to go if our boiler breaks?" asked Danny, fidgeting with Dart.

"Not with us, that's for sure." said Shannon while shoveling food into her mouth.

"Shannon!" her mom erupted.

"Just kidding Mom."

"What's in the envelope Mom? Christmas card for your boss?" joked Kate.

"How about instructions on how to smile? That would work for old Ludlow," said Rory.

Colleen sent Liam the subtle smile he loved. "It's just some plans for . . . for a new shade."

"Here mom it needs a stamp," said Danny placing one of his Santa stickers on the envelope.

"Thank you, Danny," said Colleen, placing a kiss on his cheek.

■ ■ ■

Liam and Nora sat alone in the kitchen. The dumbwaiter rumbled like distant thunder as Flann labored at the ropes, lowering bags of garbage down into the cellar.

"Safe for me to go home Liam?"

"What do you mean?"

"I was thinking you had a patrol car go over to checkout my story," said his sister flatly.

"I wouldn't do that." A cover, not a lie from Liam.

Nora lit a cigarette and took a deep drag, sucking in the smoke, and then flushing it out through her nostrils. Another toxic puff shot smoke rings toward a window framed with curtains featuring a Frosty the Snowman motif.

"Was Ernie home, Liam?" she asked.

"No, he wasn't, and the heat is still off."

"I have no idea where he is. That's the truth, Liam."

"It has to stop you can't go on like this," warned Liam.

"It wasn't always this way. You remember when Ernie and I had a life. But yeah, I know what I have to do and I'm going to do it. You've done so much I hate to ask you this."

"It's okay, Nora, what is it?" Liam skipped any cop talk. He cared about her.

"I need a few days back in Brooklyn. Can Shannon stay here?"

"Of course. That would be fine. Not a problem."

"That means everything, because I'm getting a job, and I'm going to get myself cleaned up, and more good news I'm moving back to the Heights so Shannon can be around her cousins."

Nora's words pierced him like a spear, but Liam didn't flinch, his armor was always on. "You're going to do what?"

"I'm moving back to the Heights as soon as I get a job," she repeated, "the sooner the better."

Liam pulled a smoke from his shirt pocket. The faithful zippo spit sparks and refused to light. Nora smiled and slid a book of matches across the table, feeling useful at last.

■ ■ ■

"Hey Kate, are you really going to read that entire law dictionary?" said Rory entering Kate's room, holding a copy of *Pro Football* magazine.

"I like to finish what I start, Rory," said Kate focused on the dictionary.
Rory settled in on the floor. "Where are you up to?" he asked.

"Letter F."

"F as in what?"

"F as in *facio ut des.*"

"What is that, a law?"

"A concept, Rory. I'll read it, and you see if you can apply it to something."

"Go ahead, snap the ball I can't wait. I'm beside myself with anticipation."

"Okay. *facio ut des.* That's Latin."

"I know it's Latin. Wasn't I an altar boy for five years?"

"Just checking," said Kate.

Kate placed the law dictionary in her lap and read toward Rory. " 'I do that you may give.' A species of contract in the civil law, which occurs when a person agrees to perform many things for a price specifically, either mentioned or left to the determination of the law to set a value on it; as when a servant hires himself to his master for certain wages or an agreed sum of money."

Rory turned his attention back to his magazine. "I never said I was Perry Mason."

"Think about it, because it really makes sense. Think about Flann," said Kate.

"I'd rather not," replied Rory.

"What Rory, think?" said Shannon from behind the John Gnagy pad.

"Bug out Shannon," replied Rory.

"Flann is a plumber an electrician a custodian. He collects the rents and shovels the sidewalk when it snows. But he gets one paycheck, right?" quizzed Kate.

"Of course, be dumb to pay him every time he did something. He knew that when he took the job."

"Bingo! *facio ut des.* Brilliant."

"We ought to become lawyers, Kate. Dunn and Dunn, we'd make a great team."

"Maybe you guys could give me a job." Shannon sounded concerned.

"Court artist, Shannon. The job is yours," said Rory.

"What job do I get?" Danny was not about to get passed over.

"That's an easy one, Danny, you get to fly our private plane. Right Kate."

"Sounds good to me."

Danny stood on a rainbow cloud of paint drippings captured by a white bedsheet, content with his job offer. The police shirt smock, a drape that hung from his shoulders to his ankles, had become a collage of paint wiped from his hands and Kate's brushes.

"Do you like it Kate?" he asked.

Kate turned toward the makeshift easel where Danny's current creation stood on display. Jars of red, green, brown, and white paint intermingled traditional with a neoclassic - Santa on his sled pulled by a rocket ship.

"It's beautiful, Danny," said Kate.

"I thought so too," Danny replied.

"He's so modest," Shannon said with a hint of a smile.

"Yeah, we call him Michael Angelo," quipped Rory beginning to do pushups.

"It's not for the refrigerator," Danny announced as he wiped his hands across the cop shirt, "it's for the empty door."

"There's no room left on the refrigerator," said Rory.

"You mean apartment twenty-one?" said Kate, folding up the drop cloth and stuffing it under her bed.

"For the little lady. For her door."

"We can't just put something on someone's door Danny." Rory collapsed on the floor and looked up. "She might not want anything on her door."

"We could ask her, and ask about the snow she said to believe is coming," said Danny sincerely.

Numbered pencils flew in and out of their box as Shannon sketched things that entered her head, Salt White and Plum Purple and Shannon's favorite, number 24, Pond Green.

"What little lady?" Shannon's full stomach and a warm night's sleep had restored her inquisitive nature.

"That would be Miss H. Wellington Grimes." Rory began to slink on the floor toward Danny, who stuck a finger in each ear in a futile attempt to block Rory's eerie voice. "And the reason she has those burlap bags on the windows is because she boils dead pigeons and casts spells. She's a witch all right. The worst kind of witch!"

"What kind is that?" asked a more than frightened Danny.

"Stop it, Rory, you're scaring him," warned Kate.

"The Buckingham Witch. The British brought her over to cast spells on the American troops. Right up the street at Fort Tryon Park."

"She's not a witch," Danny moved quickly to Kate and did his best to be brave. "Flann says she's a dwarf, and I know witches are tall and green and if you throw water on them they melt."

"I like the kind dressed in white who travel in giant bubbles," said Shannon as she drew.

"Is that why you keep a water pistol under your pillow? Is it because you think she might be the Buckingham Witch? I think you are playing it safe Danny Dunn. You know what?"

"What?" asked Danny, half hidden behind Kate.

"I think that's very smart. Very, very, smart."

"I think you're very, very, dumb Rory. I think you should be on your way to your precious football practice," said Kate defending her little client, while holding his hand.

"Come here Danny." Rory sat Danny on his knee, "Who's the best linebacker in New York?"

"Sam Huff number seventy New York Football Giants," Danny said confidently.

"And who is the second-best linebacker in New York?" quizzed Rory.

"Rory Dunn number seventy All Hallows."

"Right again. And do you think the second-best linebacker in New York would let anything happen to his favorite little brother?" Rory looked over his shoulder, "or his sister or his cousin?"

"I hope not," said Danny.

Rory leapt from the floor and easily lifted a squirming Danny into the air, "I wouldn't and now I have to be off because our sister is right. Football practice is precious." Rory tossed Danny onto the bed, and he landed next to Kate's Melinda.

"Can I see what you've been working on Shannon?" asked Rory.

"She draws what comes into her head," said Kate, liking Rory again.

Shannon held up the John Gnagy learn to draw pad. "Do you like it?"

Rory took a step closer to Shannon trying to disguise his shock. "That just popped into your head?"

"Yep." said Shannon admiring the spider with pond-green eyes and salt-white legs and a snowflake on its back.

"A Straw Spider!" exclaimed Danny.

"What's a Straw Spider?" asked Shannon.

"Well, in two days it will be Straw Spider day and believe me you'll hear all about it," said Rory.

Liam's baritone voice rang out from the kitchen. "Hey, you guys, just heard on the radio that it's snowing in Chicago."

"Snowing in Chicago? So what?" Shannon went back to work on her new project.

"The weather comes from the west. Uncle Weatherbee says want to know what the weather will be like in New York, look at Chicago," said Kate.

7

AFTERNOON, FOUR DAYS BEFORE CHRISTMAS.

Colleen clutched the secret manila envelope under her arm. She waited for the light to change surrounded by a dozen pedestrians laden with bags of groceries and Christmas presents. After the number three bus lumbered past belching clouds of black diesel smoke, they ferried themselves across Saint Nicholas Avenue. Mrs. Ludlow freed her ten minutes early, with the understanding she would make it up tomorrow, so she had plenty of time.

Colleen would look ridiculous running so she opted not to - but she wanted to. She wanted to run and cheer at the top of her lungs, "The Dunn's did it!"

Yes, thought Colleen, *running was out of the question, but walking fast would be acceptable.* She walked so fast that she might as well have been running and that made her laugh, first to herself and then aloud. She adopted Danny's brazen attitude about dancing on the corner and did not give a hoot about what anyone thought.

Without breaking her gait, she slowed just enough to drop the change from her coat pocket into a cardboard brick chimney guarded by a frozen Santa Claus who stood ringing his bell.

"Merrily Christmasessss," slurred the Santa warmed by Four Roses antifreeze.

"A very Merry Christmas to you too!" shouted Colleen over her shoulder.

Scores of Christmas trees planted in front of mom and pop shops had dwindled down to a precious few. Rory had reported the day before that the five trees Pedro had left were in their final stages of negotiation.

Pedro remembered the gifts the Magi brought and so he kept three of his nicest trees in the basement of Smith's hardware store. He gave them away on Christmas Eve at eleven o'clock to the children of families who had fallen on hard times and then headed to Incarnation church with his wife Layla for midnight Mass, feeling good about himself and Christmas.

Colleen wished everyone could feel as good as she did, but she knew that was impossible. No one could be as happy as she was at that moment. She kept up her quick step and made it back to 177th Street just as the lamp-posts flickered to life.

Liam would have seen the Stranger lurking in the alleyway next to Tip Top printing, hunched forward with the collar of his coat turned up to ward off The Freeze. He would have approached him and if he walked away, he would have followed. Instead, the Stranger slowly crossed the street and gazed upon the blinking Christmas lights Flann strung around the door illuminating the number 650. If detective Liam Dunn walked out of his building at that instant and faced the Stranger, he would have become befuddled and he would have had many questions, after he had caught his breath.

8

A FLYING PIG.
DANNY MEETS JOHNNY BLAST.

The trickle of light that survived the journey from the third floor fell upon Flann, who was performing his electrician duties while balanced on the top step of a rickety ladder. One last cranky, arthritic twist of his wrist brought the new bulb to life, generating a surge of light that shattered the darkness and illuminated the stairwell for Kate, Danny, and Shannon. Satisfied, Flann commenced his descent, conquering one rung at a time and filling the air with a metallic hymn sung by the choir of keys dangling on his hip.

"Hi Flann." Danny marched up to Flann with his painting.

"And hello to ya Danny and I have to be askin', who this might be?"

"That's my cousin Shannon." said Danny happily. Making introductions was one of his specialties.

Flann, who never missed a chance to harvest information, probed Danny. "Shannon, it 'tis? And what a fine name to be carryin'. Shannon Dunn, I'm guessin'?"

"Shannon Downey from Brooklyn," said Kate ending the cross-examination.

Flann knew they could not be venturing far clad in sweaters, but he was not about to have passengers wandering the decks of 650 without reporting to their captain. "And where might ya be headin', Danny, and with such a fine work of art no less?"

"We aren't going anywhere, because we're already there," explained Danny.

"Where?" Flann carefully inserted his pipe between the two teeth in his lower jaw.

Danny tapped on apartment twenty-one. "Here!"

Danny moved closer to his sister, goaded by the sound of a groaning door. Grimes's black- turbaned head slowly poked out, like a rabbit emerging from her hole, checking for a fox. She pushed the heart shaped glasses up the bridge of her nose with a hand shielded within a white glove. She reassured herself with a quick look at the ceiling before she hazarded a step on to the landing.

Kate stole a first look at Grimes removed from her raincoat. The red rubber boots scaled her shins and touched the hem on a blue velvet skirt. A galaxy of rhinestone comets glittered on her white sweater and formed a letter T accentuated with a twirling tail that caressed her shoulder. Danny presented his painting to Grimes and watched as it morphed into a mural in her minuscule hands.

" 'Tis a fine painting Danny Dunn has created and let me be introducin' ya to Miss Shannon Downey, visiting 650 from Brooklyn," said Flann, acting like an emcee.

Grimes stroked Santa's forehead as if she were feeling for his temperature. "I like the idea of the rocket ship Danny," said Grimes.

Danny hesitated, before making his confession. "I'm not very good at drawing reindeer, not yet, anyway."

Grimes raised the glasses revealing her hazel eyes, one of which, the left, drifted lazily off center, startling Danny. "It's a beautiful gift Danny and I shall always treasure it."

Kate and Shannon taped Santa on the door of apartment twenty-one bringing it to life and complementing the Christmas tree on apartment twenty-two and the nativity scene that covered the entire door of apartment twenty-three.

"Please come into my car," invited Grimes.

"What car?" Danny asked.

"Oh, did I say car?" Grimes sounded bewildered.

"For sure, ya did," said Flann.

"I guess I'm still getting accustomed to the apartment," said Grimes apologetically.

"Actually, we have to be on our way, but thank you very much for the invitation," said Kate.

"You are not afraid of me, are you Kate?"

"Of course not," said Kate. Even if she were afraid, just a little, she would never admit it.

"I was, but I'm not now," boasted Danny.

Grimes looked up at Kate. "People are often frightened by things they refuse to try to understand. Do you find that to be true Kate? And Danny, I always see you with your plane. I have something I think you would enjoy. Come with me, all of you, into my . . . let me say it correctly. My apartment."

"Please, Kate," pleaded Danny.

■ ■ ■

Boxes, stacked from the floor to the ceiling created a musty canyon that left barely enough room to trail after Grimes.

An ensemble of lamps that wore black shades, cast an eerie blend of shadows upon the walls and ceiling a clever display arranged by Grimes, who positioned her lamps on scruffy steamer trucks, plastered with decals that proclaimed the places they had toured.

Grimes combed through the menagerie of cardboard seeking the something she wanted to give Danny like a busy bumblebee flitting about pollinating a garden. Kate watched her miniature neighbor, who now resembled an ant toting a giant crumb from a picnic blanket, lifting one box and placing it on another creating a scaffold. Grimes anxiously looked toward the ceiling. "Let me see, I'm sure the aerial department was in this room."

"Miss Grimes, may I ask you a question?"

"Certainly, you may, Danny. My goodness. A child without a question is like a robin without a nest."

Danny took a deep breath and spoke as quickly as he could. "Why do you keep looking up at the ceiling?"

"I'm sorry Miss Grimes," apologized Kate, "It's really none of our business."

Flann converted a box into a seat. "I was wondering the same thing, Danny. Is there something up there we should be knowin' about? Because I'm thinkin' there might be."

"Yes, I do look up, and I do wish I could stop. I have tried. I try each day to end it. But as you can see I have not been very successful." Grimes climbed down and sat in a rocking chair that belonged in a dollhouse. "You see, Danny, I spent my entire life in the circus."

"You did?" said an astonished Danny.

"That makes two of us," Shannon softly mumbled.

A smile came to Grimes' face. "Now, about my looking up at the ceiling. The answer is quite simple. Had you worked in the center ring of the big top beneath people flying overhead, you would be looking up too."

Danny snapped to attention. "I'd be looking up and looking out!"

"I imagine each of you are wondering why I have this lovely T on my sweater."

"Not me. I have lots of stuff with other people's names on it," said Shannon.

"Would anyone like to guess what the T stands for?"

"Tiny?" speculated Danny.

"I'm sorry. Maybe we should leave," Kate apologized again.

Grimes expelled a laugh that sounded like a chirping bird. "No Danny, but it certainly would apply. It stands for Thumbelina. That was my billing. Thumbelina. The world's smallest woman."

"How nice." Kate plopped down with a loud thump on a box labeled *Books*, dwelling on her nun name.

Grimes began to rock in her chair. "As for you, Flann, you will find I am no trouble at all. Especially when the snow comes and you have to answer for the Straw Spiders you have been speaking of and not about all these years, spared by the lack of a Christmas snow in Washington Heights."

Flann thought it best not to strike a match within the tinderbox of cardboard and held his unlit pipe in his hand. "So, you were Thumbelina in the tent and Miss H. Wellington Grimes to the rest of the world."

Grimes gently rocked with her hands clasped in her lap; content to tell the story she enjoyed recounting and told with the same reverence Flann bestowed on his Shiloh.

■ ■ ■

Private Lester Grimes, survived The Great War. He returned from the Western Front in 1918 with both arms, two legs and the majority of his wits. Prior to his service in the war he completed five years of formal education at Detroit public school number eleven and labored ten years as a coal miner.

Johnnie Three Feathers, a title given to him by his drinking buddies because of his ability to consume large amounts of a whiskey by the same name, was Lester's best friend. He told Lester that his employer, Thunder Slaughterhouse, a death mill in Dearborn Michigan that overlooked the Lackawanna River and served as a slop sink for discarded animal parts, was hiring. The slaughterhouse operated like the army in which private Grimes had served in that the few commanded the many, who executed the butchering. Like the army, the men worked until ordered to stop, which was twelve-hours a day Monday through Saturday and four hours on Sunday.

Lester had some recollection of the events that ended his tenure with Thunder Slaughterhouse. He had been working on the gutting line when an explosion went off in his head. He had just inserted a fourteen-inch blade into the entrails of a four hundred-pound Texas long horn and he remembered he had been thinking about asking Elizabeth Moskowitz to a picture show. Three days later, he awoke in Dearborn General Hospital. A nurse informed him that a two-hundred-pound pig, destined to become center cut pork chops, threw itself off a conveyor belt that led to a decapitating machine. The event shut down the production line for twenty minutes and cost four men their jobs.

The long horn, relieved of its ribcage, converted the carcass into a cushion that absorbed the weight of the pig and Lester's head. The sad truth that Lester played no part in the pig's decision to take flight meant nothing. The slaughterhouse's policy was clear and concise; an accident resulted in termination of the employee. The owner of Thunder Slaughterhouse made a diligent effort to treat his employees in a better fashion than the raw material they processed. The pigs, the steers, and the cats that vanished into a sausage grinder. He paid Lester's medical expenses and included an extra day's pay in Lester's termination pay of fourteen dollars and twenty-four cents.

The company doctor told Lester he could remove the brace from his neck by himself after ten weeks, which he did. Unfortunately, a disturbing medical issue refused to resolve itself. Absent the brace, Lester's head fell to the right, settled three inches above his shoulder, and remained that way. And so Lester would forever view the world from a perpendicular angle. Other than the fact that it was difficult to keep a hat attached to his head he could function in a world that paid little attention to such peculiarities because it was 1929, a year when misfortune was in abundance.

The brokers of Wall Street, whose heads were properly facing, were busy throwing themselves from the rooftops. The country had fled from the boom years of the Roaring Twenties into the unwelcoming arms of a crippling economic depression. The veteran, of both the Great War and Thunder Slaughterhouse, made his way to the train yard, where he intended to hop on anything heading south. That train turned out to be the home of the Guilloche Circus.

Sam Guilloche, the owner and ringmaster of the circus, understood people with deformities and employed a flock of medical oddities who resided in the last two cars of the circus train. Lester presented Sam with a dilemma when he asked for work.

The tilted head sitting on his shoulder was not hideous enough to qualify him for a position in the freak show. It would have been better if the pig or war inflicted gruesome facial damage had relocated his nose or an eye, or perhaps flattened his head. Instead, Lester's rather pleasant face was intact; people were quick to acknowledge that when they took the time to tilt their own head at a right angle and gaze into Lester Grimes's eyes.

Things were looking up for Lester, even though he was unable to execute such a feat. There was a roustabout, responsible for the needs of the animals. He fed them, washed them, plucked them, and saw to their overall well-being, as Sam did for the occupants of the last two circus cars.

On the eve of Lester's arrival, the roustabout blundered by placing himself between the rear end of Atlas the elephant and the steel cage that housed a half-dead tigress, named Kitty by the clowns. No one feared Kitty, a harmless beast who could no longer roar, a feline, barely able to swat a fly. But even a tigress close to death and deprived of her natural surroundings since birth, can still muster up the strength for one final hunt. The roustabout's head, a savory casserole pressed against the bars, rejuvenated Kitty and she quickly consumed the roustabout from the neck up, not pausing for a second to consider if the head was medium rare or well done, or required a dash of salt.

The deceased roustabout's job became Lester's, along with a firm warning from the proprietor of the circus to never make the same mistake. Lester was to respect the tigress, as if she were still the ferocious monster depicted on the canvass billboard hanging on the side of the big top tent. Lester assured his employer he did not intend to place his head between an elephant's ass and a tigress's mouth. Lester thought that would be like a private first class attempting to enjoy a meal while sitting between a brigadier general and a sergeant major.

Sam knew within hours that he had made the proper decision concerning the employment of Lester Grimes, private retired, United States Army. He could pitch tents, never complained about the slop served twice a day on the food line, and more importantly followed orders without question.

A quaking, rattling, smelly, cramped box on wheels, became a home for Lester and he was grateful for it. The occupants of the last two cars accepted him. They never judged him harshly, even though his mediocre deformity did not raise to the standard of separating a paying gawker from his ten cents, five of which became their salary. Lester slept on an upper bunk, with his head resting on a lumpy pillow, placing it in the same direction as everyone else. A feeling of belonging he could not achieve while standing soothed him. Crab Man, who was born with two claws instead of hands and fingers, informed Lester what stopovers the train would make. The first would be Hathaway the last in Raymondville, Sarasota, Florida.

The train arrived in Hathaway, which was a smaller than small town, with one doctor who had married the only schoolteacher. The general store functioned as the post office when it was not the funeral home and was all that remained of Main Street.

The ringmaster offered Lester a dollar, half of what the undertaker wanted to dispose of the abandoned baby Lester discovered on the steps of the last car of the train. She was smaller than the kewpie doll prizes no one won after investing a penny to spin the numbered wheel at the entrance to the midway. Everyone, including Lester Grimes, predicted the baby's death would arrive before the sun rose.

"Was' it the freaks from the last two cars on the train who saved ya?" asked Flann.

"Yes, but they were never freaks to me even though that was what my family was called including me."

"And how 'tis it that Wellington finds itself on the lease of apartment twenty-one?"

"Lester Grimes never married, but he did have a wonderful woman in his life, the widow Wellington, who had a dog act. She filled in as a substitute mother. A very difficult situation, being a part-time mother to me and a full-time mother to the dogs. Lester was my father as far as I was concerned, and he assigned the widow the task of answering girl questions that he knew the answers to but felt uncomfortable answering. He did not want to wed a woman with nine dogs and informed her that he would pay her for services rendered, but widow Wellington would never take a penny."

"A kind soul for sure."

"She was Flann. She was very kind. I honored them both. I took the name H for Hathaway, my birth place, and Grimes for my father and Wellington for her acting like a mother."

Grimes went back to work climbing from box to box. She stopped, applauded herself, and began happily digging in a trunk. She held up a brown leather-flying helmet with glass goggles. "Here you are Danny. This belonged to Johnny Blast, the Human Projectile."

Danny pulled the goggles down, and his face became enshrined in two sheets of glass that sheltered half his face. The leather straps hung on his chest and brushed his Roy Rogers belt. He cleared himself for takeoff and flew about with his arms out stretched on a reconnaissance flight with Johnny Blast his trusted copilot. He soared off, disappeared into the kitchen, and exclaimed in the loudest voice Kate had ever heard from her little brother, "Look what I found!"

The jolliest of machines sat atop a wooden crate, and it flabbergasted Danny. Whoever drew the original plans and carried them to the patent office was certainly a brilliant somebody. These machines could be found wherever people gathered to forget their troubles, planted at the zoo or a traveling carnival or a stuffy church fair, where the vicar gave in to temptation and indulged in a quick sticky lick. They composed a wonderful opus that was not the least bit annoying, like an electric humming bird. The operators of the machines possessed the same culinary skills as the crown chefs of Europe, since they too could tickle the taste buds of their patrons. The silver tub of the machine, with a magic motor, converted sugar, that wonderful food, into a puffy cloud hugging a paper cone.

"Save us all, 'tis one of those candy cotton contraptions!" said Flann poking his head in the door.

Everyone laughed, Shannon the loudest. "Cotton candy Flann," she said.

"Like the one at Palisades Amusement Park?" asked Danny.

The machine *was* like the one at Palisades Amusement Park, the one nestled in the booth with gigantic plastic lemons hanging from the rafters. Kate loved the fresh cotton candy and a fresher cup of cold lemonade even more. Whiffs of heated sugar and squeezed lemons converted to a magical cologne that swam with the scent escaping from the world's largest salt-water swimming pool and returned with Kate to 650 and boarded in her room, seasoning her dreams for weeks.

But amusement was the furthest thing from Kate's mind when the subject of the thirty-acre thrill park sitting on the cliffs of Fort Lee New Jersey was the topic of conversation. Incarnation School made a trip to the park an annual June event. The excursion took place on a Wednesday, nickel ride day.

The Cyclone Roller Coaster was a rite of passage in Washington Heights. For a boy to weasel out of going on the towering scream machine was unforgiveable, exhibiting a total lack of the body parts that separated him from the girls. Kate had already passed through the maze of winding steel bars that managed the long line and was waiting to get on the ride when she observed the ridiculous chipmunk, a rodent altimeter, holding out its paw.

Luckily, for Kate, double-scoop-head Beatrice Smith and her best friend Sandra the Lisp Humphrey would reach the height station well before Kate. The sixteen-year-old boy working the ride was more concerned with a teenage girl pressed into a pair of short-shorts and was paying no attention to the height of the ticket holders. Tom Thumb could easily have traipsed aboard the Cyclone.

Sister Mary of the Crucifix happened by on her way to the motor boat ride that circled the park, a pleasant cruise that required no nautical skills, a ten-minute escape for the nun from the crowds and a chance to sneak a quick Salem cigarette. The nun saw no need for the chipmunk or the teenage height monitor whose testosterone levels had reached the boiling point. A simple order from her would solve the problem.

"Incarnation School students line up by-size places right this instant!"

Sister Mary of the Crucifix patrolled the line in her flowing black habit like a penguin searching for a hole in the ice, ensuring that the students of

Incarnation School obeyed as quickly as if they were in the school building. Suddenly, Kate found herself standing behind Beatrice. Beatrice would be a sacrificial lamb, like Faye Wray dangling in front of King Kong.

"Move up," ordered the nun now in total control. Beatrice took three solemn steps, as if she were walking the plank of a pirate ship and placed herself under the wooden paw. "Short. Next."

But there would be no next. Kate walked away with her friend Mary, who would have easily strolled past the glorified rat. This year's failure was not Kate's concern. It was next year's and the year after that and the year after that. She could care less about the ride. It was the ominous lines on the dumbwaiter and those stubborn hidden lines in Mary's room that filled her with remorse and anger.

In the kitchen Grimes climbed atop the steamer trunk, placed her hands on either side of the silver tub and studied her audience.

"I believe it is going to snow today," Grimes's voice took on an air of authority, "Danny, do you believe?"

"I do Miss Grimes. Oh, yes, I do believe it will snow," said Danny who believed in all that was good as he climbed up on a box next to Grimes.

"And you Shannon?"

"I'd rather it snows on a school day." Shannon believed in practicality. "Kate?"

"Kate believes, don't you Kate?" asked Danny, his words full of hope.

Kate looked upon Danny, and for three seconds he became – frozen in time, as if The Freeze had invaded the kitchen in apartment twenty-one, and a flash bulb popped in her mind capturing his face, framing it within the leather-flying helmet. She took a love-filled step toward her little brother who smiled and looked down from his cardboard pedestal next to Grimes.

"Danny," said Kate, "At some point, it will snow. And since it's snowing in Chicago I guess that yes . . . I believe snow is possible."

"Well I will accept possible as a very good start, yes, very good, Kate," said Grimes, "But now gather around. You too, Flann." They watched as

Grimes removed her glove and ran her index finger around the silver tub glazing her finger with crystalized sugar.

"Hold out a finger," said Grimes. Each guest pointed a finger at Grimes and she softly touched each one.

"Now like me." Grimes touched the tip of her tongue, igniting a smile on her face. They all touched the tip of their tongues, and they all smiled.

Grimes jumped off her box and scurried about the kitchen looking for this or that and not finding it. She placed her hands on her hips and studied the floor, but nothing seemed to enter her mind.

Then she placed her index fingers on her temples just below the turban and took a deep cleansing breath. Danny stood at attention hoping that whatever Grimes wanted to happen would happen.

"Of course!" Grimes moved a box to the counter next to the refrigerator and climbed up. Kate thought she resembled a toy on a shelf at the Doll Hospital on Broadway. Tiny chirps emerged from her throat confirming her discovery, a cereal size box that looked like a small suitcase in her hand. Flann stepped forward and extended his hand to Grimes.She paused, tilted her head, and studied him for a moment quietly assessing his gesture and began her descent with the box securely in her tiny hands. "Thank you, Flann."

The cotton candy machine sprang to life and filled the kitchen with its happy hum. Danny stood on the box next to Grimes. The Johnnie Blast glass googles began to fog up from the heat of the machine and so Danny lifted them to the top of his head.

"Are we ready?" Grimes asked.

"We are!" Danny was ready, Shannon was too. She had not enjoyed so much food since a dinner at the Salvation Army. But Shannon's mother forbade her from ever talking about that day or the meal.

Grimes opened the top of her box and poured the contents into the machine. Within seconds some zillion pellets began to spin around in the silver tub. Grimes picked up a paper cone that became a magic wand in Danny's mind and expertly moved it around and around with the rhythm of the machine.

Suddenly, without warning, like a summer thunderstorm, a puffy cumulus cloud of cotton candy appeared. Bigger than the ones at Palisades. Bigger than the one at the Bronx Zoo. The cotton candy confection was ten times the size sold at the touring carnival that pitched its tent in the vacant lot on 176th Street and stole the coins of every child in Washington Heights trying to win a twenty-four-inch Schwinn bike.

Grimes handed a delighted Danny his cone. She spun another for Shannon whose happy face became stickier than flypaper. Suddenly, three solid raps from the steam pipe rang out. "That's my friend Mary," said Kate.

Grimes turned off the machine and jumped off her box. She ran to a drawer, and pulled out a wood spoon, that was almost as big as she was and handed it to Kate.

Flann watched Grimes toting the spoon that looked like a shovel in her hand, all the while knowing that her message, like all the messages in 650, would travel steel pipes and wind up in his room in the basement.

"May I, Kate?" Grimes asked.

"Sure, go ahead, knock two times," said Kate walking to the window.

Grimes tapped the steam pipe twice. Kate carefully pushed aside a burlap bag curtain and lifted the window, which sent a salvo of frozen air into the kitchen.

"Kate look! It's starting to snow!" Mary's voice bounced around the alley.

It was just a flurry, so slight that Kate thought Mrs. Stern from the top floor was shaking out her dust mop. She snaked her hand through the window guard and watched a snowflake kiss the tip of the finger glazed by Grimes, and then the flurries disappeared, and the alley filled with the lonesome wail of a distant police siren.

9

STRAW SPIDER DAY.

Flann stood on the stoop, a proud Celtic drum major, tapping his varnished shillelagh on a stone step as if he were the Pied Piper himself surrounded by the Straw Spider class of 1962. There were three children from 660 and five from 670. Representing 650 were Danny Dunn and Third Floor Sean, a name bestowed by Kate that removed the confusion with Sean O'Leary from the second floor. The candidates arrived with their older brothers and sisters who carried their own Straw Spider chests, because that was the tradition, and tradition mattered to Flann McFarland.

They paraded north on Broadway, snickering at The Freeze, and then veered toward the Hudson, where the sorrowful drone of the traffic cascaded from the George Washington Bridge and created a never-ending lullaby for the tenants residing west of Broadway.

Danny obediently blessed himself as he walked past the chapel where Mother Cabrini slept within her glass shrine as the sun played a game of tag with the clouds, appearing, and then disappearing. The leafless trees lining Flann's parade route looked down on the troupe as they neared the Cloisters, which stood like a castle protecting Washington Heights. Knights in medieval armor stood their watch within its gray limestone walls, guarding treasures that made Westminster Abby look like a poor-house. That's what Flann had to say, and anyone who visited the Cloisters agreed.

Kate savored the Cloisters in the springtime, when the fumes from exhausted coal furnaces vanished, replaced by the scent from the hon-ey-suckle planted along the stone paths that wove through the grounds. Content in her solitude and comfortable on her bench, she studied her law dictionary, awash in the sound of Gregorian chants.

■ ■ ■

Flann leaned on his shillelagh and waited for his breath to return. Feeling restored, he slowly continued his way up the cobblestone road leading to the Cloisters, a twisting road he first trekked forty - six Christmases ago, when the Irish walking stick was a prop, not a cane, when his back was straight and his vision sharp, when his heart was the property of Cara Dwiggins.

Cara Dwiggins arrived in America shortly after Flann and found her-self ten steps ahead of the other Irish immigrants because she had a job waiting, thanks to Finola, her older sister, a maid who worked for a wealthy textile merchant. The woman of the household, Victoria Greystone, liked Finola because she was efficient, spoke when spoken to and even more im-portantly, kept her distance from the master of the house Mr. Greystone.

Jacob Greystone considered himself a righteous individual who lived his life accordingly. He did not drink and disliked those who did. He did not smoke and believed people who used tobacco lacked self-discipline. He was an Elder at the First Presbyterian Church on Fifth Avenue where he installed the finest pipe organ in New York City and hummed joyfully along with the choir on Sunday mornings. He demanded respect from those who worked for him and those who competed against him on both sides of the Atlantic and he received it.

The current Mrs. Greystone was in fact the second Mrs. Greystone. Mrs. Jacob Greystone the first was still alive, which was a testimony to the flawed matrimonial presumption of, "until death do us part."

Victoria did supersede death and began her employment innocently. What transpired between herself and Mr. Greystone was not a one-sided plot. She simply reminded Jacob that he was still a man, four years after he had relinquished such thoughts. Jacob's attorneys agreed to the terms set forth by his wife, and she quietly left for her twelve-room villa on the Costa del Sol. He learned two weeks later that the minister of his church had joined her and that they were happy together and her lover was tending to a new flock.

Victoria had little concern as to what people thought of her. Her attention centered upon what people thought of her husband. Especially female people. Specifically, female people employed by her husband as she had been. She discharged the stunning Julianne Reynolds, the cousin of the chef, who resembled Cleopatra arriving on her barge three hours after she stepped foot in the French marble center hall of the Greystone residence on Central Park South.

Finola wasted no time in assuring Victoria that Cara would make an acceptable addition to the staff. Victoria contemplated Finola's request for a moment and then presented her proposal. "Your sister may have the position. If it doesn't work out, you will both be gone."

Young Flann climbed from the darkness of a manhole and stood squinting in the September sun for five seconds. When he regained his sight, Cara Dwiggins came into focus. A life-altering encounter on the corner of 57th street, where the handsom cabs waited to take riders into Central Park for a ten-cent trot around the lake.

She must be domestic help of some sort, thought Flann; she did not have the look of a sweatshop. Her shoes were from home, he was certain of that. He had seen a thousand pair, black leather with brass eyelets. However, they were never on the feet of anyone as beautiful as Cara, or as kind or as gentle. Flann had not spoken a syllable to her but he knew it. Just as he knew, she would be his wife.

" 'Tis a beautiful day to be in New York City we can both be sure of that," said Flann.

Cara turned to Flann who was wiping the grunge from his hands with a rag. She lived on West 33rd street and Twelfth Avenue, in a two room flat with her sister and four other Irish women. She was careful whom she spoke to, but Flann looked harmless enough.

" 'Tis a fine day," said Cara and then she was on her way to work. But the rugged young face with the familiar brogue occupied her thoughts and reflected from her bucket when she scrubbed the floors.

The Shovel Shit and Shovel brigade was at work installing electric ducts, a job that would take months to complete. Flann kept his nineteen-year-old face shaved and did his best to keep himself presentable.

He waited for Cara every morning, tipped his weathered tweed cap, and gave a polite hello. After a week, he mustered up the courage to invite her to a free concert at the Hibernian Hall on Union Square. Six months later, they married at City Hall and pledged to each other a priest would, "wed them proper," as soon as they saved enough money. Cara erased Flann's past and paved his future and he called her, Dwiggy.

She was frail, still recuperating from the Hunger back home in Ireland when the flu epidemic shredded New York City. Thousands died, including Flann's eighteen-year-old bride. There was no consoling Flann McFarland. He spoke to no one for a year and no one spoke to him, not even Big Jim Riley. Before he went silent, he told his best friend, "Keep back Jim."

The general foreman put Flann to work swinging a sixteen-pound sledgehammer, busting out bedrock on Pearl Street, eight hours a day. He meant well, thinking it might dispel his wrath. Flann's arms and shoulders turned to iron, and he took to prize fighting.

He had no boxing skills, and when the man who called himself a manager offered him a stall in his stable of fighters, Flann walked away. He harbored no interest in the ring. His interest resided in pummeling people. He had eight middleweight fights. None went past five rounds of a scheduled twelve rounder. Flann put three men in the hospital and one in Conner's funeral home.

The New York State Boxing Commission placed the blame on the referee for not stopping the fight. Flann buried his boxing gloves in a trench and never fought again. He spoke to no one of his boxing or his Dwiggy;

no one in 650 knew of it, except for Detective Liam Dunn. He made it his business to know things about the people he dealt with.

■ ■ ■

Behind a massive holly bush, which greedily clung to its red berries throughout the year, was the secret entrance to the crypt of the Cloisters. Big Jim Riley stood like a mountain waiting for Flann with a ruddy face made ruddier by the Camel cigarette glued to his lip, a permanent fixture that he inhaled and exhaled without removing from his mouth. His baggy black pants ended short of his shoes and made his white socks a focal point, detracting from the official-looking tin badge pinned on his lapel. The middle brass button on the uniform's jacket was missing but was of no consequence because Big Jim patrolled the passageways from the stroke of midnight until dawn, observed by eyes that never blinked. Sculptured stone eyes and eyes of oil paint were his lone inspectors.

Flann and Big Jim Riley were Belfast men, which meant they knew the same poems and told the same jokes. They might have loved the same women but would not be sharing it among themselves or others. When Big Jim fell to Peggy Doherty, Flann McFarland proudly stood as best man.

Flann lit his pipe and looked fondly upon his congregation. "As fate would have it who should get the job as night watchman of the Cloisters? said Flann, not waiting for an answer he continued, "Why Big Jim Riley himself. We spent forty-five years in the trench and I'm not telling a lie when I tell ya he was as fit on the day he packed it in as he was on the day he hired out. The jewels of the Cloisters could not be in safer hands."

Kate hadn't a clue about Big Jim and Flann's ages. Seven years had passed since Kate received the Straw Spider box that she held in her hands. She studied the two and concluded that the old reached a point where they ceased aging. *Their hair can only get so gray* thought Kate. *Only so many wrinkles can camouflage a once handsome face.*

The sun paid a quick visit over the Harlem River and ignited thousands of sparklers on the surface of the water but failed to move the temperature one iota. Danny and Third-Floor Sean fought off the cold by hopping up and down on invisible pogo sticks, while yearning for the warmth that waited within the walls of the Cloisters.

"Would we be ready, Big Jim?" asked Flann.

"I'm ready," said Grimes, walking toward Flann and his troupe of bundled-up acolytes.

"And ready for what? I might be askin' ya."

"Why, for the children to receive their Straw Spider chests. Unless I'm mistaken it is Straw Spider Day, and I'm here after receiving a personal invitation from Danny Dunn."

"And wasn't that a grand idea on the part of Danny." said Flann, as he eyed Danny.

"I thought it was a very nice gesture," said Kate.

"Then we will be about our business, all the while knowing Miss Grimes, that silence is the order of the day."

Big Jim tugged on the enormous door leading to the crypt, doing a fine job of making it look like a struggle. He had loosened the bulbs in all but two light fixtures attached to the walls, which created an eerie mine shaft that led to a room where bags of salt sat stacked and a regiment of snow shovels lined the walls. Unnoticed, Big Jim sneaked off from the rear of the formation. Suddenly, the soft low voices of chanting monks filled the crypt from a hidden record player.

Flann tapped his shillelagh on the stone floor three times and removed his tweed cap, exposing a dense crop of silver hair. The new Straw Spider recipients stepped forward. Sermons belonged to the clergy, Flann knew that and made sure he never gave one. Speeches were the property of politicians, who only captivated drunks and morons, so like a skilled teamster, he steered clear of giving speeches.

The children were like puppies on a leash. He allowed them to pause for a sniff here and there and granted them time to poke their noses under a twig. But eventually, they went where Flann led them, and so it was in the crypt of the Cloisters on Straw Spider Day.

The Straw Spider chests were identical, made by Flann from cedar, with crafted tongue-and- groove slots that interlocked tightly and required a gentle tap from his mallet to complete the job. A comfortable chest, content on a young lap, painted gold, so the children believed their chests to be fourteen karats and found a haven for them under their beds. A brass clasp fastened the cover so that the Straw Spider would not find itself disturbed.

The Straw Spider, whittled from oak and stained white by Flann's friend Jack Curry, resided inside his chest, napping in a cradle of glittering tinsel Flann called Christmas Straw and nestled beneath a quilt of parchment that appeared as ancient as the Dead Sea Scrolls. As each Christmas passed Kate became more convinced that the paper appeared coffee stained and the edges looked as if a match seared them. But for Danny Dunn and the class of 1962, the Dead Sea was very much alive.

"There will be no question askin'. The Straw Spiders will be accepted as they are," warned Flann, "If anyone of ya and I'm referring to this years honored recipients - if any of ya are wondering whether what ya are about to hear is truth or lie or rumor or fact let me know now. And the same will apply to Miss Shannon Downey visitin' the Dunn's from Brooklyn. Past the age of six she 'tis but that's not bein' her fault and so she too will be presented with a chest."

Silence smothered the crypt, like a church when the priest performing the wedding asked if anyone present had a reason not to proceed to the exchanging of rings.

There wasn't a Catholic or Protestant living room in Washington Heights that didn't have a place of honor set aside for the crèche portraying Mary and Joseph admiring their child, surrounded by the working folk, the shepherds, and a sheep or two purchased for an extra dollar. Standing back, looking in at the goings on, were the three wise men, Balthazar, Gaspar, and Melchior. They brought with them gifts of gold, frankincense, and myrrh.

Unbeknownst to them, they would receive a gift as well and that became the first exchange of Christmas presents, according to the gospel of Flann McFarland.

Kate promised herself she would not ask questions, regarding the Magi or the Straw Spider story. She would obediently keep her assessments to herself. She glanced at Shannon sketching on the John Gnagy pad and watched as Mary roamed the perimeter of the room, clearing her nostrils with firm blows and discreetly slipping the tissue into her Straw Spider chest.

"Balthazar was the first to present himself," Flann began. "He was the youngest of the Magi and because he was the youngest he forgot his manners and stepped in front of the others with his frankincense." Flann's pipe became a thurible of pipe smoke.

Kate silently gnawed the inside of her mouth. It was right there in her encyclopedia. The Magi were twenty, forty and sixty. The splendor of youth, the maturity of middle age and the wisdom of the elder. Balthazar was the oldest and brought myrrh.

"And what might Balthazar see?" asked Flann. *Nothing*, thought Kate. *More than likely he was as blind as a bat.* She buried her face in her hands.

"Balthazar knelt down and what should he see but a spider. He reached out and picked up the spider before it could create a problem for the new family.

Then Gaspar knelt with his myrrh. And what might he see?" asked Flann puffing on his pipe, "Why a spider, sittin' before them takin' the best seat in the house in front of the holy Manger. Gaspar looked at Joseph and got himself a firm nod lettin' him know it was all right to be takin' the bug."

Kate twisted a strand of hair around her finger and tugged on it until it hurt. She knew spiders did not have antenea; they were not insects.

"When it came to be Melchior's turn," Flann continued, "he presented the gift of gold which drew a loving smile, the only kind of smile that could come from our Blessed Mother."

Kate began to gnaw on her knuckle. Melchior was the middle child of the Magi and brought the myrrh.

"And when he brushed aside a bit of straw to place his gift of gold what should he see but a spider. Right there sitting on a leg of Baby Jesus' manger," said Flann.

"A Straw Spider?" The words fell out of Shannon's mouth like a loud belch at the dinner table and caught everyone's attention.

"I'll continue now without any questions if yer not mindin'," said Flann. He picked up a canvass sack that Saint Nicholas would have been proud to own and removed the Straw Spider chests. "The Magi returned to their own lands with their spiders safely packed in chests aboard the backs of their camels. The gift to the Magi was that the spiders found in the straw could grant a wish. A Christmas wish. Only granted if it snows while all the Christmas trees in every home are still standing – decorated and lit. But with that power they lost the ability to spin their web."

Flann began to hand out the Straw Spider chests to the class of 1962 along with solemn instructions. "You will give your Straw Spider a name and ya will whisper that name to it. But you will never let anyone know this name, for if ya do, your wish will be denied. If it snows, each of ya will be required to spin a web, anywhere you like of anything that ya choose. If you're findin' yourself in any luck at all, your wish might be granted."

Flann took his time relighting the pipe and scanned the children, making sure he held their attention. "Now for the most important part of owning a Straw Spider chest."

Danny could not contain his curiosity and lifted the lid to peek in his gold chest. "Danny Dunn be payin' attention now," warned Flann before he continued. "If your wish were granted take your Straw Spider chest to church and place it in front of the manger. This allows for someone ya do not even know to have a chance for a Straw Spider wish."

Flann looked toward Kate and removed the pipe from his mouth and said, "This is how it must be and the way it shall be. Tell me now, all of you, by saying 'I accept this chest and understand what I must do.'"

"I accept this chest and understand what I must do." Kate whispered the words for Danny's sake. Like she did with the cookies on Christmas Eve. And the key that allowed Saint Nicholas to miraculously enter homes with fire escapes not fireplaces. Kate contemplated her web. If it snowed, it would be the best. Like her award-winning power plant.

10

THE WISHING BENCH.
DANNY BREAKS THE
ELEVENTH COMMANDMENT.

Gifts inter vivos: A Latin phrase meaning gifts between living people. Kate closed her law dictionary and cuddled it on her lap like a purring kitten, content with herself and thoughts of Christmas gifts. She watched Shannon who remained immersed in a drawing frenzy that had begun when her mother departed for Brooklyn. She drew birds and insects, and when people became her subject, she hid their faces within shadows cast by leafless trees with distorted broken boughs. She focused instead on their hands, drawn with the skill of an artist years her senior.

Shannon slowly sharpened pencil 8, Desert Sand. Pleased with her effort, she closed her eyes and blew upon the point, as if she were making a wish on a birthday candle, and then gently placed it back in the box. "Do you know where you're going to high school?" she asked Kate.

"Sure do," said Kate firmly adding, "I'm going to Sacred Heart of Mary. Everyone calls it SHM."

The school, shaded by towering oak trees, sat nestled atop a hill on the northern tip of Manhattan. Kate had decided in seventh grade, after attending a book fair, hosted by the nuns of SHM, that she would attend the school and that she would graduate as valedictorian.

Kate slid a catalogue from under her pillow. "You want to see the uniform?" she asked. Shannon knew she was going to get a look no matter what answer she gave.

"Sure," Shannon politely replied.

"Actually, we have two uniforms, one for winter and one spring," bragged Kate.

Shannon glanced in the direction of the catalogue and espied a beige jacket. Another blazer, navy blue, appeared more formal, with a plaid skirt with matching knee-high socks.

SHM was expensive, but that did not concern Kate who qualified for a full academic scholarship. The pride of Incarnation achieved a perfect score on the entrance exam. The other applicants fretted about the essay question. Kate possessed no such fear. She composed an essay, concerning the Holy Trinity, that was so compelling and written with such eloquence, that the cardinal himself ordered it read from the pulpits throughout the archdiocese of New York City. Katherine "Kate" Dunn never thought about where she would spend the next four years. Kate always said, "It's a Dunn deal." She knew, everyone knew, she was going to the Academy of the Sacred Heart of Mary.

Kate watched Shannon slowly turn the pages of the catalogue. Remorse, suddenly overwhelmed Kate. Her shame became a walnut wedged in her throat. Her eyes brimmed over with tears. Kate berated herself. *How could I have shown Shannon the catalogue? Shannon has nothing. Shannon has Ernie. On a good day, he could put his pants on.*

Kate's escape route from her shame was beneath her bed. "Why are you going under the bed Kate?" asked a bewildered Shannon. Kate retreated into compose mode and took deep breaths.

"Kate," said Shannon looking under the bed, "what the heck are you doing under the bed?"

Kate eked out a response. "I ah … I thought I put some records under here." There were two forty- fives, Bobby Vinton and Frankie Avalon.

Kate closed her eyes and continued to take deep breaths. She scaled the imaginary stairwell in her mind, to her roof, her oasis, where summer memories waited. Once again, as on starlit nights, the beacon on the George Washington Bridge swept the night sky, passing over Kate every four seconds, a intricate part of the celestial world she cherished and as dependable as Polaris. The Big Dipper, forever reliable, overhead. Orion's Belt, where it belonged, never askew, hovering over the dome of Lowe's movie theater. Each piece of heaven was a part of Kate's personal planetarium. She wandered among a rooftop of urban scarecrows, those friendly gray antennas were securely attached to televisions by a web of wire that hugged the brick skin of 650 like a waterfall, with outstretched arms that received those mysterious signals that radiated from atop the Empire State Building.

Danny flew into the room. He froze in place, remembering the Eleventh Commandment taped to Kate's door: THOU SHALT NOT ENTER THY SISTER'S ROOM WITHOUT KNOCKING.

He lifted the goggles on the Johnny Blast flying helmet and waited like a submarine commander for the first depth charge to explode.

"Where's Kate?" asked a cautious Danny.

"Can I tell him Kate?" asked Shannon.

Kate exhaled the summer and regained her composure. "First, he has to ask for forgiveness and he knows why."

"I'm sorry Kate. Why are you under your bed?" queried Danny.

"You are forbidden from asking any questions for the rest of the day. That is your penance for violating the Eleventh Commandment. Consider yourself lucky! The Great Oz has spoken," said Kate in the deepest voice she could muster.

The sound of sleigh bells and a hardy voice singing "HO-HO-HO!" resounded from the front door and filled apartment thirty-one. Danny spun around and Kate quickly scurried from underneath her bed.

"Grandpa Finn!" Danny exclaimed.

■ ■ ■

Everyone, including Bridget his wife called Finbarr Dolan Finn. The couple was a set of bookends, one as short as the other. Kate inherited their

short gene that had evaded her mother and brothers. There was no denying it. Kate accepted it and loved her grandparents despite it.

Grandpa Finn had spent forty years laboring on the docks, a long-
shoreman who called The Freeze, "a nip in the air." He confronted it with
a weathered tweed jacket kneaded like his face by decades of snow and rain
into a flaccid stick of butter that drooped from his once solid frame. His
Irish sweater, in spite of Bridget's care, had yellowed with age into a summer sunset that stubbornly clung to what remained of its warmth and hid
all but the knot of the red tie he wore at Christmastime.

The four-block walk, from their apartment on 173rd Street and the
climb up three flights of stairs, caused Grandma Bridget's breaths to arrive in short spurts. She settled down on a kitchen chair without removing
her coat and waited patiently for her lungs to catch up with her heart.

Grandma removed her scarf. It was long enough to engulf her head
and coil around her neck. The two Santa Claus barrettes that Kate had
bought at the Five and Ten Cents store three Christmases ago held her
thick silver hair back from her face. Her wire-rim spectacles, which allowed her to see the ground beneath her feet, perpetually slid down her
nose and required her constant attention.

The grandparents had survived the Great Depression and lived their
lives buying things they needed, not that they wanted. Kate grew up hugging her grandmother's frayed wool coat, and, unlike her own mother, had
no concern about the three mismatched buttons or the brown shoelaces
on her black shoes that she repaired with simple love knots.

Grandma spoke little about her past. Bridget Clancy escaped the hunger and despair of her homeland and never looked back, not so much as
a quick glance over her shoulder. There was not a dish or spoon from
"the other-side" in her kitchen, no Clancy family portraits, or sentimental
knickknacks to share with her grandchildren or hang on a wall when she
finally found herself a home.

What she did have, to pass on to her daughter, was a bookmarker, a farewell present, from the priest who visited Ballymena twice a month and celebrated Mass in a field that was once the property of her great-grandfather,

before it became a gift to an English colonel. Intricately stitched with The Lord's Prayer, it became a Christmas ornament on Colleen's tree.

■ ■ ■

Christmas week delivered a forest of trees, rooted temporarily on the fire escapes of Washington Heights. The Freeze spun a cocoon that kept their sappy branches supple and sealed their pine scent.

The Tree from Pedro's Corner would not leave Kate's fire escape without the supervision of her grandpa. That was the Dunn tradition, even though his age reduced him to a referee moving about the ring, important but ignored by the crowd. Liam passed The Tree through the window to Rory who took hold of it as if it were the opposing team's quarterback and maneuvered it around the bed and through the French doors.

"You ladies have that tree stand ready?" Liam's cop voice bellowed from the bedroom, all but drowning out The Little Drummer Boy blaring on the hi-fi record player that Colleen had redeemed with Plaid Stamps. Rory stood with The Tree on his shoulder. The two inches in height and the ten pounds he added since last Christmas, chipped away at the boyish look Colleen missed and helplessly watched slipping further and further away with each passing day.

"Did you remember to put the aspirin in the water?" asked Grandpa.

"Kate please get the aspirin," said Colleen trying to be nice.

"What? The tree is sick?" asked Shannon looking up from her pad.

"Some people think it keeps a tree fresh," mumbled Kate, heading toward the bathroom.

The Dunn kitchen became a bustling Christmas workshop. Rory and Liam untangled and tested strings of lights hastily packed away along with last year's Christmas memories. The task of finding elusive loose bulbs went to Danny and Grandpa.

Like Sherlock Holmes and Doctor Watson, Danny and Grandpa nosed about, checking each bulb. Grandpa's nicotine-stained fingers led the way and loosened every other bulb, which guaranteed little Danny's expert attention, earning him the fair wage of a dollar.

Grandma watched Kate and Shannon free a trove of ornaments trapped in shrouds of tissue paper. Mr. and Mrs. Claus and their army of elves and translucent gold balls and crystal angels and a ensemble of rag dolls Colleen had created from scraps of fabric swept from Mrs. Ludlow's shop floor made their appearance. Colleen kept her special ornaments, created by her children, in a shoebox. Christmas wreaths, woven from red and green wool, became picture frames for school portraits under the watchful eye of Sister Elaine, everyone's favorite Incarnation teacher. Rory in third grade with his head trying to catch up to his new primary teeth, and Kate's wreath, the wool taut and neatly glued, with her second-grade face locked in a determined stare down with the camera.

"A Christmas Jingle," composed by Kate in sixth grade was in the fancy frame Liam had purchased in Donahue's Irish gift store. It became a holiday ritual for Kate to read it on Christmas Eve.

> *There was a man named Santa Claus,*
> *who went from house to house. He slid*
> *down the chimney and oh my jiminy*
> *the fire was not put out.*

> *By Katherine Dunn. Class 6a 1960.*

Colleen unwrapped the miniature park bench Liam had constructed from toothpicks and paper clips. Awarded a place of honor, next to the bookmarker and was the last adornment she placed on The Tree. Unlike the bookmarker, Colleen shared with no one the story of the little bench. Instead, she waited for her family to fall asleep to sit with the bench on her lap and return to her youth.

■ ■ ■

The experience was most unexpected, very intrusive, and thoroughly misunderstood, an undiagnosed disease of the heart that quickly metastasized to the respiratory system, a stealth shoplifter that pickpocketed the breath of fifteen-year-old Liam and left him totally exhausted.

He knew it was her fault, because prior to her intrusion, his life was, as it had been five seconds earlier - happy and unconfused. The girl, whoever she was; Liam had not a clue, created this frightening earthquake without uttering a word, without as much as a glance in his direction.

The mysterious girl had a kite and a good day to fly it. She came with her mother and father who served as ruckus cheerleaders and a little tyke of a brother, who chased a flitting butterfly in an ever-expanding circle. She wore a red skirt, a blue turtleneck sweater and a black beret that sat jauntily cocked to the side of her head. Tucked into her tennis shoes were a pair of bobby socks, an adolescent must-have, in 1938.

Once Liam rescued his heart from the grass, he began to follow her, all the while keeping a safe distance, along a winding path that passed Grant's Tomb and ended on Riverside Drive. She paused and draped her hair around the nape of her neck like a muffler. Liam watched her drink from a stone water fountain. Three minutes later, she boarded the number four bus with her family and disappeared, leaving Liam with the task of learning to breathe again.

Liam often returned to where the kite flew and the butterfly flitted. He ventured back until the wind washed away an ocean of autumn leaves and laid bare hordes of industrious squirrels preparing for winter. He returned to the park in the springtime for baseball practice. He became a star shortstop, and stole as many hearts as he did bases. The days and the weeks slowly passed until his search for the girl ripened into an occasional glance.

Two years later, seventeen- year- old Liam pedaled his Good Humor ice cream bike down the shady path the girl once walked and she was there. Liam came to a frozen stop, as solid as his bestselling Italian cherry ice. He slowly peddled behind her until she reached a secluded bench. Liam's tongue began to thaw, and when it did, he asked if she might be interested in a strawberry ice cream cone. After all, Liam explained, they were on sale, half price, and a bargain at three cents.

They met each day that summer at the bench, and Colleen soon became Liam's business partner. She rode atop the ice chest and rang a string of bells that attracted a colony of sweaty children and handed out napkins to the happy customers.

Liam and Colleen did the things that new lovers did, planning each day to ensure they shared every possible moment. Old dreams yielded to new, jointly owned ones. Then the newsreels began to appear, on the screen of the RKO theatre on 181st Street. They picked at their popcorn in silence and watched Europe burn and their dreams and the dreams of all of those they knew - became nightmares.

Colleen read the first three letters Liam wrote while sitting on the bench. When they continued to arrive, she considered it a good omen and decided to read all his letters there. Colleen baptized it the Wishing Bench, and carved those words into it.

Colleen's wishing for Liam's return lasted from the winter of 1941 to Thanksgiving of 1942 to the Fourth of July 1943 on to Christmas of 1944 and ended in February 1945, when Liam fell wounded for the second time, on an island called Iwo Jima.

■ ■ ■

Liam evicted the TV from its corner and stepped over a spider web of extension cords and antenna wire to prepare a place for The Tree. Thirty days ago, it had remained an unnoticed pedestrian deep within a Vermont forest. Now it presided majestically over apartment thirty-one, dwarfing Liam's frail mohair chair, a pal that Colleen would replace if he let her.

When the "Christmas electricians" completed their tasks, Liam wove the lights among the branches, ensuring each received a fair share of holiday illumination. The bubble lights, dancing court jesters, were the last to adorn The Tree. Liam tactfully secured each liquefied electric candle so that it stood perfectly straight. Little Danny patrolled from one to the other, a general inspecting a dazzling display of multi – colored, boiling ornaments.

When Kate dimmed the lamps, The Tree exploded into a kaleidoscope of light that pranced on the walls and ceiling. Colleen reprised her role as Liam's supervisor when he crowned The Tree with their gold star. She recited her instructions like a psalm that she delivered each Christmas in her calm prayer like voice. "A little to the left Liam, no a little to the right yes, that's perfect."

11

SHOPPING WITH FLOATING CORNFLAKES.

"There be so many candy stores in the Washington Heights. I'm telling you Miss Kate - even more than those fire hydrants." Kate knew that was not true, but on 177th Street Pedro's assessment was almost true. There were three fire hydrants and two candy stores. Rory called them refueling stations where a continuous flow of playful customers drank, licked, and chewed, pounds of sugar.

Kate's Christmas shopping began at Stan's, the candy store next to Jack Kelly's law office. Stan Schultz, the owner, was a plump gruff old German, who barked his accented words with an unlit cigar, which he gnawed, more than smoked, stuck in his mouth. Stan knew that people called him, "The Kraut" behind his back. To deflect this unsavory alias, he mounted a picture of his oldest son, Stan Junior in his army uniform, over the cash register, hoping it would remove any doubt as to where the Schultz family lined up during the war.

Stan sold the biggest salted pretzels for two cents, instead of three and his customers sipped a nickel egg cream in a ten-cent size glass so business was always good. He orchestrated all that went on perched atop a milk box behind a counter surrounded by mountains of candy, the most expensive and popular strategically displayed up front. Babe Ruth, Three Musketeers, Laughing Chuckles, and bricks of Turkish Taffy. Pocket size bags of M&M's and fish bowls filled with a choice of Bazooka or Double Bubble gum that sold for a penny that sat next to boxes of Milk Duds, Kate's favorite.

Music filled the air in Stan's Candy Store, but it didn't come from the radio. It was a musical, performed daily, between Stan and his short order cook Jackson, pronounced by Shultz as "Yack-son" and echoed by all the kids on the block.

"Yack-son! Gimme' da' fish on rye and put da' wings on it!" Tuna to go.

"Okay, Yack- son, come on. Gimme' two and mess em' up." Scrambled eggs

"Gimme' me da' sunrise Yack-son and hold da' meat." Sunnyside up no bacon.

"Gimme' da' actor on a roll." Ham sandwich.

Jimmy the Jerk, a name that had nothing to do with his mental aptitude; delivered the outgoing orders Yackson put "wings" on. In the summertime, Kate sat with Jimmy, who people guessed was at least forty, solving crossword puzzles. Kate did the writing because Jimmy's entire body jerked in uncontrolled spasms every thirty seconds. Detective Dunn did a background check and was comfortable with the results. Jimmie was another harmless soul who had washed ashore on the streets of New York City and somehow managed to survive.

His conditioned improved when he met the High Spot bartender, Mike Hickey, who prescribed a steady dose of Fleishman's whiskey, which made the jerking occur every two minutes, but caused Jimmy to walk like a crab returning to the ocean, a protracted sideways path, back and forth across the sidewalk.

Stan enforced the NO READING sign he posted over the comic book rack like a tyrannical librarian. He kept the dirty magazines on the top shelf, out of the reach of curious altar boys who hung around until they ran out of the few cents in their pockets. Kate picked out three of Rory's favorite comic books. *GI Joe*, *Blackhawk*, and *Superman*. Thirty-six cents.

"Do you know what else you are going to get?" asked Shannon.

"If it's for Rory she does," said Mary, Queen of Snots, wiping her nose.

Kate knew what her brother would enjoy discovering under The Tree. She had bought him packs of football trading cards when he turned fifteen in July. He almost hugged her. Rory savored opening them, quickly handing off the paper-thin bubble gum to Danny. He removed one card at a time. Chicago Bear. Not a problem. Washington Redskin. Respectable. Despised Baltimore Colt. Another despised Baltimore Colt. Rory sighed in utter disbelief. A third despised Baltimore Colt. Redemption came with the last card in the second pack. New York Giant fullback Joe Morrison. The Giant card went into Rory's "never trade" stack. The Despised, Respectable and No Problem cards Rory used for flipping and trading went into his Straw Spider chest, a haven for the cards.

Kate bought five packs; twenty-five cents. A new addition to the football cards section, next to the jars of licorice surprised Kate. The ballpoint pens with the Giants logo cost twenty cents. She bought an extra one to replace the one she knew Rory would lose.

Kate removed a dollar from the metal Band-Aid container she had converted to a bank, money saved from her dollar- a- week allowance and babysitting.

"I'm going to get Danny a new plane," said Shannon. She had eight dollars to spend, three from Liam, three from Grandpa Finn and two from her mother.

Kate wanted Dart, the glider Danny planned to fly out of a window gone, not replaced, and wished Rory would never make another Scotch Tape repair. She quickly came up with an alternate gift.

"Look," Kate announced, "They have Davy Crockett cards. You hear him singing that Davy Crockett song all of the time." Shannon suspiciously eyed Davy Crocket, who was posed on the card aiming his musket.

"He loves Davy Crockett," repeated Kate as persuasively as she could.

"Dart is broken," snapped Shannon holding a fifty- cent plane in her hand; it had a bigger wingspan and a rubber band engine that powered its propeller.

Kate was not about to yield on the plane she hated. "I heard my parents talking Shannon. They are getting Danny a new plane. I'm sure they already have it." Kate would have to confess the lie that was not a cover sin, next time she went to confession. Shannon reluctantly returned the plane to its spot on a shelf and picked up the Crockett cards, which made Stan chew harder on his cigar.

The snow forecasted to arrive in Washington Heights by way of Chicago, called in sick over Lake Michigan, which ended the thoughts of a white Christmas and granted Straw Spider wishes. That made the unanticipated microscopic flakes falling outside Stan's Candy Store, and dancing around Kate, Shannon and Mary even more miraculous.

The Freeze had prepped the ground for three weeks. Everything stuck; it appeared that Kris Kringle himself was emptying a saltshaker over the streets of Washington Heights dusting the coats and hats of shoppers. The tease of a snow quickly matured into giant cereal-like flakes, floating to the ground, as if they were pieces of a jigsaw puzzle, falling into place on the asphalt roadways, turning the sounds of the city into a muffled murmur. The storm became a surprise Christmas present, with each flake a relished gift ecstatically unwrapped by the children of Washington Heights, a welcome situation that meant everything they did would evolve around snow.

The snow quickly accumulated on the sidewalks, and the older folk began shuffling instead of walking, with invisible skis attached to their feet. Kate watched Mary being silly in a way that Kate finally accepted as amusing; walking in a slow circle with her arms outstretched, flicking her tongue like a hungry toad at falling snowflakes. Shannon, who was learning to laugh again, joined with Mary and, because she was a novice, caught a flake on the tip of her nose. *Snow,* thought Kate, *brought about the oddest behavior.* She watched her cousin moving around the street, like a venus fly trap attempting to snare an elusive flake.

"Come on," Kate called out, "The store is going to close."

Costello's Religious Gift Shop was next door to McDonald's Funeral Home and across the street from Incarnation Church, an ideal location for gifts that soothed suffering souls. Carmelo Costello burned the incense and lit the candles he sold, making it the holiest of stores, where both the shoppers and the merchant spoke in hushed voices, as if they were in church.

Carmelo had no competition in Washington Heights. He did not concern himself with who was selling an egg cream in what size glass or the going rate for a piece of Double Bubble. Carmelo set the market. A ten-inch plaster statue of the Blessed Mother: six dollars, eight dollars, if it came from a Vatican studio. Jesus with his heart exposed: ten dollars. Jesus with a lamb over his shoulders: twelve dollars. Carmelo thought it would appear sacrilegious to tag Jesus "on sale," and so nothing in the Shop found itself discounted, ever. Certainly, not on Jesus's birthday.

Mrs. Carlo, from the Delicious Fourth Floor, told Kate that Carmelo and his wife were not real Italians as she was. She came from Salerno; they were from Sicily. Grandpa warned Kate not to trust any Italian, which he pronounced "Eye-talian," and said if she married one, he would never speak to her again. Colleen's brother did marry an Italian and Grandpa never spoke to him again. Uncle Connor moved to California with his wife Maria and worked for TWA airlines. Kate had two cousins she had never met but from the photograph he enclosed in the Christmas card he sent every year, it appeared they evaded the short gene.

Despite her grandpa's warning, Kate's last conscious thoughts, the past three months, before falling asleep, focused on Frankie Romano, Rory's teammate, a quarterback who lived on 172nd Street. Kate intended to marry him after she graduated from law school. She wondered what would bother Grandpa more - a lawyer for a granddaughter or an Eye-Talian calling him Grandpa.

Grandpa told Kate when she was eight years old that she could not marry a heathen Prod either. She looked it up in her dictionary and told Grandpa a prod was a stick used to move cattle. Rory had to explain to Kate the difference between Protestants and sticks.

The cloud of incense failed to overcome the smell of the simmering tomato sauce laced with garlic and oregano that Mrs. Costello stirred in her kitchen in the rear of the shop. The sauce and the incense greeted the girls and at the same time confused their senses. Carmelo wore his priest like uniform every day, a black suit, black shirt, black shoes, and black socks. All that that prevented his ordination was a white collar. He strummed his stubby fingers on the glass counter top as if he were playing a pipe organ. "Such a' lovely young a' ladies' comma' into my store. I'm a' such a' lucky man," he said in an accent that blended perfectly with the aroma of his wife's cooking.

He stood surrounded by sets of rosary beads and crosses of every size with chains of gold and silver. Hand-sewn vestments, separated by iconic paintings of Jesus walking on water and of Jesus feeding the multitude, hung like tapestries from the walls. The shoppers took off their mittens so they could point out a potential gift.

"So tell a' me Kate, how is a' your Papa?"

"He's fine." That was her answer. It never varied. After his transfer to the Narcotics Division Liam called his children into the kitchen. He told them in his cop voice, not to discuss his schedule with anyone. Kate could have missed that Dunn assembly. She never discussed anything with anyone concerning her father even before the transfer.

"He's on vacation," added Shannon. Shannon did not know the rule. Kate would change that.

"That's'a' good thing. Officer Dunn he a' hard workin' man. He's a' keepin' us a' safe."

Kate thought a statue of the Blessed Mother would look nice next to her parents' wedding picture. Mary wanted a Saint Christopher medal for her brother Andy, who was leaving for the Navy right after Christmas. Shannon was not sure where or whom she would be spending Christmas or with whom so she was undecided.

Mary studied the medals. "This one looks very nice," she said, pointing to a round silver medal.

"That a' good a' choice," said Carmelo approvingly.

"It's for my brother; he's going in the Navy. Saint Christopher would be good."

"Oh, this is a' not the Saint Christopher. This is the a' Saint a' Jude. He be the saint for losta' cause when there is a' no hope. Your brother he be fine you will see he will come a' home with lots of stories about the places he a' went to."

"Could I see that one please?" asked Shannon pointing to the Saint Jude medal.

"Sure, if you want a', here is a' Saint a' Jude."

"It's very nice," said Shannon examining the medal for causes she understood.

"Saint a' Jude the hopeless saint comes with the nice chain."

"Can I see the statue of Mary? The one on the second shelf," asked Kate.

Carmelo placed the statue on the counter. Kate liked the rich red color of the Blessed Mother's robe. He turned the statue upside down to show Kate the shiny new penny that would bring good luck taped to the statue. Kate immediately set the Blessed Mother on her feet and pointed out the tiny chip on her toe.

"I have a' little paint I can a' fix it right away."

"My brothers have lots of paint, so we can fix it. But I do think a discount would be fair," said Kate.

"Yeah, at least two dollars off," said Shannon.

"I a' take off a dollar and give you a' nice a' box."

Kate led the way out of Costello's with the Blessed Mother tucked under her arm. Saint Christopher swam in a pocket full of tissues in Mary's coat. Shannon held Saint Jude, Patron of Lost Causes, firmly in her hand, while darkness and snow fell on Washington Heights.

The unannounced snowstorm, a glorious meteorological Christmas present continued. Kate could not see where the sidewalk ended and the road began. She checked her watch, a gift from her grandparents last year that had replaced the Tinkerbelle watch she had stopped wearing. It was five – fifteen. Kate would have to call home. That was her father's rule, even if she were only going to be ten minutes late. Shannon and Kate pulled on the frozen phone booth door. It surrendered after three hardy tugs. Kate dropped two nickels into the phone and waited for the dial tone.

"Hello," Rory answered the phone.

"It's me."

"How about this snow. And no one even predicted it."

"No one except the Grimes woman."

"Yeah. I forgot about that."

"Ok, listen; tell Dad we are on our way home."

"Can't. He went out. I'll tell Mom."

"He went to work, didn't he? They called him in." Kate did not attempt to disguise her concern. Her father called to work, while on vacation, meant something was going on.

"Take it easy Kate. Dad said he was going to meet his partner. Probably have a beer for Christmas." A cover for Liam from Rory, who did not reveal he saw their father strap on his backup snub nose .38 ankle holster.

12

OMEGA.

The Zippo erupted like a flamethrower illuminating the interior of the unmarked car Liam shared with Carlos Rodriguez; the thirty-four-year-old had ten years on the job, seven working narcotics. Rodriguez was the most decorated detective in the division, a fact known by no one outside of the NYPD. Rodriguez's award ceremonies took place in the commissioner's office. No reporters. Liam and Colleen always showed up, along with a few other cops and Rodriguez's wife, before they divorced.

"What do you say Dunn? How many steps do you think you could take down the street before they figured out your lily-white ass is attached to a cop? It's like me being grand marshal at your Saint Patrick's Day Parade. This shit just doesn't work. But I give ya credit Dunn, I really do." Rodriguez said.

"I can't tell you how much that means to me Rodriguez. Funny you should bring it up, because I put your name in the hat for grand marshal. And I think I can find a pair of kilts that might fit," replied Liam with a friendly mockery.

"How'd I do?" Rodriguez asked.

"It was so close they're doing a recount," said Liam as seriously as he could.

"If I win, Dunn? Tell ya what. Your days in the back of the Irish bus are over. I'm gonna let you march up Fifth Avenue right next to this Puerto Rican. How about that?" Rodriguez laughed and took a hit on his smoke.

"Jesus Christ, Rodriguez I don't know how I'll ever be able to repay you for that."

"I'll think of something," said Rodriguez. His attention latched onto three kids walking toward the car pulling sleds. One stopped and cupped a handful of snow from the stoop of the target building and made a snowball. His two friends watched as he went through his pitching motion before throwing a strike at a fire hydrant.

"They're on their way to the park," said Liam.

"Hope so."

The cops watched the boys trot past their car, sleds in tow. The street was dark. The same team of federal agents, who tapped the phone line had disguised themselves as utility workers and dismantled the lamppost in front of the building three days ago. Blue Christmas lights, strung haphazardly around the front door blinked in a perfectly timed sequence every five seconds, illuminating the stoop and falling snow.

They knew the target. Omega: a codename for Tyrone Petersen, aka Tire Iron, after his weapon of choice, was in the building. There were no footprints on the stoop. No one had entered or left since the snow began to fall in earnest three hours ago. Two additional cars parked at either end of the street would begin to advance in four minutes. Liam took a hard drag on his cigarette and watched his partner Powers, a black cop, shopping in the bodega across the street with Detective Laura James. A believable cover, husband and wife stopping for a loaf of bread and a quart of milk.

The fictitious husband and wife, Lionel and Cynthia Bradshaw, had become Omega's neighbor two months ago, using a rented U-Haul and with two cops posing as friends helping with the move. They made sure Omega's cadre of bodyguards, posted at the front door of the building became familiar with their faces. Powers made a point of making small talk and asking for a light so they could get a good look at each other.

Powers hated the drug dealers who were invading black neighbor-hoods and the politicians who were doing nothing to stop it, other than giving a speech or two when they thought it would glean a vote.

Liam and Powers arrived in the Narcotics Division on the same day. Liam immediately noticed the USMC etched on Powers' right forearm. Wounded in Korea at the invasion of Inchon, Powers returned to his unit and then survived the brutal battle at the Chosin Reservoir. Liam's war, fueled by revenge for Pearl Harbor, ended in victory. But Powers, fought in a "police action" that lasted three years, cost 33,746 American lives and ended in a stalemate. Like the war on drugs.

Omega ran his operation out of the second-floor apartment. His neigh-bors in Fieldstone, an enclave for the rich in The Bronx, believed him to be a legitimate businessman with his two car washes, a bowling alley in New Jersey and two bars in Brooklyn. All these were money-laundering operations that provided a steady source of income to pay drug peddlers working the school-yards, corrupt cops, their bosses, and half of the City Council.

One of the guards, posted inside the building walked toward the bo-dega where Powers and James were shopping. *Perfect,* thought Liam. *Two cops will take him down as soon as he exits the store.*

The Bradshaw's were glad to see the guard. "Hey what's happening man?" said Powers.

"Nothing much. What you been up to?" The black bodyguard had Powers by three inches and forty pounds. Powers was glad the thug in front of him had become the gofer.

"Me? You know workin' for the man, tryin' to stay outta' trouble."

"He best be behavin' if he knows what be good for him." Detective James used her pick on her perfectly shaped Afro. She was in her second year of night law school and could turn her street dialect on and off at will. The guard could not take his eyes off her. He had been trying to bed Mrs. Bradshaw since the day after she moved in. "The soup is something else. Ain't I right honey?" she asked.

"I love that soup," said Powers. The heat from inside the bodega cre-ated a thick curtain of frost on the window that blocked the guard's view of his post.

Powers smiled as he exited the bodega with James. He could hear the guard say. "Yeah, let me have two roast beef on rye bread. And two of them soups."

Powers body slammed the one guard in the vestibule down and hand-cuffed him while James taped his mouth shut. Liam rushed through the door, followed by Rodriguez and a platoon of cops. Everything was going according to plan. Two cops held a ramrod, which would breach the front door. Surprise and firepower would take over. Suddenly, there were shots from the street. Powers knew the crack of the first round fired was not from a cop .38 caliber pistol. But the second and third were. Powers figured the massive bodyguard was not interested in returning to life on Rikers Island.

"Go! Go!" yelled Liam. The cops rammed the front door, which withstood the assault.

Omega blasted the door with a twelve-gauge pump-action-shot gun. The cops dove for cover. Omega dragged a Christmas tree out of the living room. He lit a newspaper, stuffed it in the tree, and shoved it against the door.

The apartment rapidly developed into an inferno, forcing smoke into the hallway. When the door finally yielded and flew open, it heaved a wall of flame at the cops whose focus turned to the innocent tenants trapped in the building. They raced from floor to floor banging on doors and carried the old and the children down the stairs out to the street.

Omega slid down the dumbwaiter rope into the basement, where Detective Powers was waiting, backed up by Dunn and Rodriguez.

"Can you smell him? I can. He's here. Always has that cologne on." Fire truck sirens blended with Powers's words as the trucks rolled up in front of the burning building.

Omega had a problem. He had dropped his weapon down the dumb-waiter shaft. It landed in a pit ten feet below the basement, a rat's nest with no access to it.

Omega knew the cops were in the cellar. There was no way they would leave it unsecured. He placed his back against the wall, slid to the floor, dropped his head between his knees, and studied his crotch.

"What's going on, Tire Iron?" said Powers. He held his weapon up and moved along the wall.

Liam and Rodriguez lay down on the concrete floor, waiting for the fight to commence.

"I don't have a weapon," yelled Omega.

"No weapon?" Powers continued to advance. "Well maybe Santa will bring you one. You been a good boy, Tyrone?"

"Kiss my ass, you pig cop," snarled Omega.

"Come on now, is that anyway to talk to your neighbor?"

"Up yours!" screamed Omega.

"Here's what you are going to do. You're going to come out with your hands in front of you. If I don't see your hands, I'm going to blow your worthless brains out. Tell me you understand your situation."

"I'm coming out." Petersen aka Tire Iron crawled out of the dumb-waiter room. Water from the hoses fighting the fire began to flow down the walls forming a river on the floor, soaking his clothes. Powers placed his boot on the drug dealer's neck while Rodriguez cuffed him.

■ ■ ■

Melinda kept her vigil perched upon a pillow between Kate and Shannon, who slept with the Jon Gnagy pad and pencil number nine, Cranberry Candy, clutched in her hand. The thunderous roar of a sanitation truck dropping its plow on to the asphalt invaded Kate's room.

The Christmas lights, woven through the window guard remained lit and created a soft afterglow that filtered through frosty windowpanes in Kate's room, emitting barely enough light to birth a shadow.

Liam turned from the bed where he stood watching the girls, and said softly, "Good night Kate."

After the door clicked shut, Kate freed her fingers from the rosary beads, crept from under her covers, and unplugged the lights. Safe, back in her bed, she tucked Melinda under her arm, and tried once more to fall asleep.

13

THERE'S NO BUSINESS LIKE SNOW BUSINESS.

The alarm clock shook Rory awake at 4:00 a.m. He pulled the clanking pest from under his pillow and silenced it before it woke Danny. The model planes, hanging above him, continued their mission, guided by a crucifix nightlight that Colleen purchased from Carmelo Costello. Danny needed the comforting light after Rory took him to see *The Curse of the Vampire*. The night-light was a reinforcement for the water pistol Danny kept loaded and ready under his pillow to confront the wretched Buckingham Witch.

Rory tugged on his jeans, two sweatshirts, the Sam Huff jersey, and then quickly coiled the scarf Grandma had knitted around his neck. He zipped up his red ski-jacket and pulled on galoshes that retained a rubbery odor that mimicked the smell of the tire store on Amsterdam Avenue. Rory moved as fast as the clumsy boots would allow, passing apartment doors with Straw Spider webs quickly spun from bits of thread borrowed from sewing baskets or mismatched nuts and bolts and scraps of wire taken from unsuspecting fathers' tool boxes.

He inched closer to Grimes' door, beckoned by a whirring sound he had never heard before. If Rory possessed the X-ray Superman eyes that Danny pretended to have, he would have observed the Grimes woman toiling at her wheel, spinning mounds of cotton candy into spools of sweet thread, a dazzling twine that she strung from room to room, a sturdy tightrope for the Christmas fairies that she delicately placed between sparkling crystal icicles.

The steam from Flann's furnace flowed through a radiator in the vestibule and hissed its loud song and dampened the air, creating a wet musky scent. The snowdrift that formed against the door, darkened the vestibule, making Flann's Christmas lights brighter. Rory stared in wonderment, captured by the magnitude of a storm that only H. Wellington Grimes had predicted. The wind, when it blew, covered the stoops of Washington Heights with sweeping marshmallow slopes. Rory set his shoulder against the door; it fought back like an opposing offensive lineman. When the door finally yielded, he treaded gingerly down the stoop, feeling for steps that lay hidden beneath the smooth unblemished snow. He gazed up at the street lamps, transformed during the night into white candy canes with their globes encased within igloos that left their bulbs struggling to find a purpose. Above the street lamps, the predawn sky presaged sunrise with a blush of purple. Rory looked up and over the rooftops, and then he smiled at a lone star, slowly bidding him farewell.

■ ■ ■

Colleen stretched her hand across the bed. It had been another fretful night, repeatedly awakened by a moaned rollcall of Marines - a litany of names belonging to men she had never met, who had died on islands Liam never revealed. Her fingers came to rest on a towel, saturated by a river of memories that waded ashore in her husband's sweat.

She slipped from their bed and into the dragon robe and draped the towel Liam slept on over a wooden chair that became an improvised indoor clothesline. Liam returned with two cups of coffee, pleased to find Colleen awake and wearing the robe.

"Rory is out making his rounds," said Liam, his words spoken in a well-rehearsed parental hush.

"No point in asking you about last night," Colleen said.

"False alarm. No big deal."

Knowing that prodding him further would be fruitless, she changed tact. "How's Powers? And I think we should invite Carlos for Christmas dinner."

"Powers is fine. I'll see if Carlos has any plans." Liam watched Colleen run her hand through her hair, knowing it always presaged a serious turn in a conversation. "We have to talk about Katherine Liam."

"She'll be fine," said Liam, savoring the first sip of coffee.

"No Liam. I'm worried. If it weren't for Mary Garvey, who would she have? You tell me, Liam, who would she have?"

"Maybe if she didn't spend her whole life with her head buried in that law dictionary she would have more friends." Liam took another sip, "You'll see; once she puts down that law dictionary she'll make some friends. What about your parents? Did you mention our plans?"

"After the holidays."

"They'll be fine too."

"And you have to tell Nora. I don't think it will be what she wants to hear, with all that's going on with Ernie," said Colleen.

"She told me she's planning on getting a job. You know, getting her life back on track."

"Well, that's good news."

"It is. It is good news and I'm happy for her. The thing is her plan includes moving back to the Heights."

"Here?" said Colleen forgetting to whisper.

"Now listen to me" said Liam in a measured voice, "we both know Nora always has plans and they rarely play out. So, for the time being let's see what she does."

Colleen swallowed her coffee, her feelings, and the cop voice.

"So, everything is on hold until after Christmas?" asked Colleen.

"Well," said Liam stroking the dragon on her robe, "maybe not everything."

■ ■ ■

The shovel Flann lent Rory was waiting by the basement door. It always was whenever it snowed. Flann knew Detective Dunn's son would be the first to begin shoveling out Washington Heights. He'd tutored Rory three winters ago on how to use his knee to push the shovel into the snow, how to spare his back and lift with his legs. " 'Tis not how much ya move in a minute, 'tis how much ya move in an hour, so be pacin' yourself, Rory Dunn."

Rory shoveled a path for Flann, clearing the stairs that led to the street and erasing his footprints. He placed the shovel over his shoulder like a rifle and marched toward Broadway. A brisk breeze whisked through the streets, reddening his cheeks and skimming flakes from drifts, dropping them once again like sprinkles falling on an ice cream cone.

Rory waded through the knee-high snow and headed for the dark windows of Kelly's law office. The garage attendants, who were busy shoveling away the drifts that attached themselves to the massive elevator doors that ferried cars to the upper floors of the garage next to 650, nodded their approval at the boy heading for a man's workday. Across the street, the Stranger, was back at his post in the doorway of Tip Top Printing.

Brian Kelly never brought a case to trial and that allowed him to say he never lost a trial, which he said loudly on more than one occasion in the High Spot Bar. His was a general practice law firm, a one-man legal convenience store. He drew up simple wills. If a rare complicated estate case presented itself, he quickly referred it to a large firm with partners who handled such estates and generated a 10 percent finder's fee. He tended to routine real estate matters for local banks that paid the rent and other operating expenses, including Monica Broome's part-time salary.

The storm delivered a beautifully wrapped Christmas gift for Brian Kelly and the lawyers of New York City, a welcome precipitation that created a blizzard of currency, personal injury lawsuits. The just rewards, for anyone who labored through law school and which determined whether the attorney's year would be a successful one.

People would, of course, fall; hopefully the event would have occurred on a well-insured sidewalk. Cars undoubtedly would skid into other cars. There would be horrific pain and untold suffering. Sworn depositions taken and motions filed in a timely manner. Doctors retained to contradict other doctors, while the healthy learned to limp in preparation for their entrance into the courtroom. Then, one hour before the trial began the insurance company would make its final offer. Brian Kelly would convince his client that the check, after expenses and less his 30 percent fee, was more than equitable. Since the offers were always larger than the amount forecasted by Kelly at the outset of the matter, the client went home content.

Because he was so familiar with lawsuits, those he filed and the potential ones against him if someone stumbled and broke a leg or an ankle in the snow, Brian Kelly wanted his sidewalk cleared first and paid a premium to ensure it happened. The small sidewalk area was a warm up drill for Rory, as simple as doing a few sit-ups. It was a job he could complete in less than an hour. The attorney's credit was good, so Rory would return on his way home for his five dollars.

The snow caused a flurry of activity. Sanitation trucks, armed with plows, cleared the roadways, piling the snow on street corners, creating the Alps of Washington Heights. A cadre of child soldiers emerged from apartment buildings and invaded the streets, busy troopers who constructed snow forts atop each peak and catapulted a storm of snowballs over white ramparts that rained down on helpless buses. The snow transformed young boys into brave squires who grabbed steel garbage can lids as shields during snowball fights. After a welcomed truce, negotiated over a Stan's hot chocolate, the lids became makeshift sleds that carried daredevil riders down the man-made slopes and across icy sidewalks.

The Christmas lights spanning Broadway flickered to life as Rory shoveled toward 181st Street, where the sidewalks widened and the pay increased. He watched as his friend Tommy dug out Patrick's Bar. Tommy's father owned Philbin's Bar and saw to it that his son had the bars of Washington Heights as his customers. Rory understood. Detective Dunn was Rory's agent and spoke to the florist, the baker, the TV repair shop, and the shoemaker concerning their snow-removal needs.

Rory's last customer was Johnnie's Butcher Shop. The butcher paid four dollars and a sandwich consisting of a thick slab of baloney, slapped between pumpernickel bread, painted with spicy mustard. It was a sandwich that Rory inhaled like a vacuum cleaner.

Water logged and exhausted, Rory entered the Chapel of Repose in the Church of Saint Elizabeth. He set his shovel down, removed his gloves, quickly genuflected, and blessed himself as he gazed upon the stained-glass window above the small marble altar depicting Christ's resurrection. Three, unspoken-for candles in front of a sandstone Pieta, waited patiently amid a flickering arcade of dying tapers. Rory dropped a nickel into the coin slot and struggled with a match to ignite a stubborn waxy wick. When the candle came to life, he attached his prayer, beseeching Mary to watch over his cop father.

Rory audited each of his pockets, he enjoyed the bookkeeping, it was the best part of being in the snow-shoveling business. The crumpled-up dollar bills in his left pocket smelled of the remaining half of the pickle he had snacked on and totaled ten dollars. The right pocket contributed another six. His inside ski jacket pocket pushed the ante to forty - five. With the five dollars Jack Kelly owed he would be only a few dollars short.

Not a problem, thought Rory, knowing he could get an advance on his allowance from his mom. He had saved enough of the money he earned bagging groceries at the A&P and carrying them home for elderly customers to complete his early shopping.

Rory had already bought two five-ounce bottles of Channel No. 5 Toilet Water. He could not understand why they named it toilet water, but that is what his mom wanted. He assumed his Aunt Nora would too. He hoped his father would like the new shaving cup. Danny would love the spaceman ray gun that fired Ping-Pong balls. Rory certainly did. He had paid more than expected for Shannon's watercolor paint set, but because she really did know how to paint, he thought it money well spent. Grandma Bridget always seemed pleased with a set of fancy handkerchiefs, so he had stayed the course and done the same for Grandpa Finn's three pairs of socks. Only one gift remained on Rory's list. He needed the snow business money to purchase it, and the storm gave it to him.

■ ■ ■

Monica Broome, Kelly's part-time assistant, was teaching herself to type. Because she continually yielded to temptation and looked down at the home keys, she blindfolded herself, which gave her teased hair the appearance of a mushroom. She held her head perfectly straight and ordered her hands to their battle stations, like a salty gunnery sergeant.

"LEFT HAND. A-S-D-F. RIGHT HAND. J-K-L- SEMICOLON."

Rory let Flann's shovel drop to the floor with a loud thump, startling Monica. She pulled off the black scarf that covered her eyes. "Oh, hi Rory. I didn't hear you come in."

"Hi, Monica, is Mr. Kelly around?"

"Ah… no he's not." Kelly had trained his assistant not to mention the High Spot Bar. "But he left something for you, I'll go get it."

Rory watched as a school of five goldfish orbiting a pink ceramic mermaid with yellow hair that blew a steady stream of bubbles. A lonely snail, who had lost its appetite for algae, allowing a green tint to display itself in the aquarium, hid behind a plastic oyster that slowly opened and shut, exposing a bogus pearl. He approached a wall of photographs with pictures of a younger smiling Brian Kelly, clad in a tuxedo and surrounded by important looking people. Between the photos were certificates of appreciation from the March of Dimes, the American Legion, and the Society for the Prevention of Cruelty to Animals that confirmed the attorney's sense of civic responsibility.

Rory performed a quick survey of Monica's desk. A potato jammed in a glass jar, filled with murky water, spawned a leafy vine that crept around her desk and ended next to a tower of file folders and one manila envelope. Rory looked closer. Danny's Santa sticker removed any doubt as to where the envelope originated.

14

WRAPPING UP PRESENTS AND 1962.

Rory awoke tired with arms that ached from shoveling tons of snow. What he had discovered on Monica Broome's desk deprived him of the peaceful sleep he was accustomed too. He would have rather roused to the pleasant fantasies of Nancy Warren, whom he was mustering up the courage to say hello to, or perhaps an intercepted pass returned for a touchdown.

He knew the envelope had nothing to do with lampshades. So, Rory scratched that off his mental list. He understood that people went to lawyers because they broke the law or stood accused of breaking the law. He understood that people brought their problems to lawyers, but he had no idea what kind of problem existed in his family. One thought, frightened him so much that he blocked it from his mind. Were his parents getting a divorce? He refused to think any further about it. The only person he ever knew, who dealt with that scary problem was Jimmy Abbot from apartment fifty-two.

His parents divorced. That was what the stoop gossipers said among themselves. Three months later, they vanished. No one knew where Jimmy and his mother went, not even 650's captain, Flann McFarland. They disappeared on a Sunday morning; no one spoke of them again, no one. Rory reassured himself that there was no chance his parents were getting a divorce because Colleen and Liam rarely argued and never participated in the protracted screaming matches that had emanated from behind the bolted doors of 650.

Rory knew his sister never would have departed from Brian Kelly's office without discovering what was in the envelope. Kate would have solved the problem. Like a song, stuck in his head, the annoying scene starring his sister played nonstop in Rory's mind.

"Hi, Monica," a friendly Kate would say.

"Oh, hi, Kate," says the blindfolded mushroom.

"I'm here to pick up my brother's money. Mr. Kelly and Rory have a quasi-contractual relationship. I know, because I am reading the entire *Black's Law Dictionary*. I'm up to letter R. As in *ratem rem habere*. That's Latin for to hold a thing ratified."

"Yes, Brian, I mean, Mister Kelly, left it for him."

"Oh, look, there's that envelope."

"What envelope?" Monica removes her blindfold.

"The one right there. With your poison ivy growing around it. Look! There's Danny's Santa stamp. How about that?"

"Yes, that is for your parents, all right. It is very important. Would you like to read it?"

"Could I?"

"Absolutely," Monica would say. And mystery solved.

Padding to the kitchen, Rory tried his best to erase the scene and instead sought a clue as to what might be going on. He focused on his mother, gliding around as if she were on roller skates- nothing. Colleen appeared as she always did, content with her children, her job, and especially her husband.

He watched Shannon and Kate who were always concocting ways to trick little Danny into revealing his Straw Spider's identity. But Danny remained strong and stubbornly guarded his Straw Spider's name and giggled while he deflected a barrage of intrusive queries. Rory resorted to quietly stirring his Rice Krispies, in a slow methodical circle, ignoring the Christmas chatter at the breakfast table. Kate, who was forever vigilant for changes in her environment, knew something was troubling Rory - before the first snap, crackle and pop ended. Her brother never buried his face in his cereal bowl, or his football Giants' dish stacked with bacon and eggs, or half a loaf of French toast. She was accustomed to his blissful face at meal times, grinning about what he said or was about to say.

Rory slowly guided his spoon from his bowl and into his mouth, a feat typically performed in nanoseconds. Kate wondered if he might have a toothache. The last thing anyone needed at Christmastime was a seat under Doctor Walberg's drill. So, even though Kate no longer believed in make believe things, she managed to make a wish. "Please, fix whatever is bothering the second-best linebacker in New York." Rory decided that he could not discuss what he had seen with his sister until after Christmas. He really wanted the throbbing problem to go away. But he decided to follow his football coach, Brother Anthony's advice. "Eat the pain."

■ ■ ■

The presents found themselves stowed in secret hiding places that experienced Dunn snoopers knew well, concealed in closets, behind pails, shovels, and inflatable toys and buried beneath beach bags bulging with bathing suits and enormous towels fragranced with suntan lotion and the lingering scent of the briny breezes of Rockaway Beach. The holiday routine was easy for Danny to comprehend when he helped Rory wrap gifts in their room: Saint Nick's helpers, everyone other than Saint Nicholas himself, purchased the boring presents, the toilet water, shaving cups, and fancy hankies, all of which required the hands of a mortal to wrap. The wonderful gifts, the toys waiting beneath The Tree, never arrived concealed within Christmas wrapping paper. Saint Nick and his helpers had no time to wrap trucks and dolls or board games and scooters. They were too busy making the toys. That is what Kate said, and Danny believed it.

The delivery of the toys, which Danny anticipated for 364 days, required no explanation. Saint Nicholas himself landed on the roof and called upon his magical key. Danny thought any child, living south of the

North Pole, which of course would include Washington Heights, knew that.

"Okay, Danny. Put your finger on the ribbon and hold it as tight as you can," mumbled Rory.

"I know how to do it." Danny pushed his Davy Crockett hat away from his eyes. The Johnny Blast flying helmet was getting a few hours off and relaxed on Danny's bed next to Robby the Robot.

Rory pulled the red ribbon, created a loop, and attempted to tie a fabulous bow, the kind moms can do perfectly every time. Then Danny quickly removed his tiny pink index finger, knowing it was not going to happen. Rory knew it too.

"Well?" Rory held up the box of toilet water and looked at Danny. It resembled a bow, hastily tied on a sneaker during a seventy-five innings, twenty-boy-per-side stickball game.

"It's better than the one you tied around the Easter Bunny's neck." A cover certainly not a lie.

"Thanks, Danny."

■ ■ ■

Liam settled into his chair and watched Rory and Danny setup their electric train, connecting the metal rails that captured and reflected the light emanating from The Tree, which danced within the room. The pine scent flowing through apartment thirty-one mingled with the aroma drifting from the kitchen, where Colleen and the girls were baking Christmas cookies. Kate and Colleen had added Shannon to their Christmas cookie assembly line. Kate rolled out the dough; Shannon pressed out stars and sleds and Santa faces. Colleen stood ready at the oven, protected in an apron with a joyous tapestry of Christmas.

"Rory. Turn on the TV, it's time for the news," said Liam. The Nightly News with Walter Cronkite, aired weeknights at 6:00 p.m. and lasted fifteen minutes. The ending story concerned itself with a country few Americans could locate on a map.

"As 1962 draws to a close, the Pentagon has reported that a total of fifty-two American servicemen have been killed in the ongoing conflict. Secretary of Defense Robert McNamara will be testifying in front of the House Armed Services Committee next week. Several members of the committee are looking for reassurance that the United States is not going to become involved in a ground war in Vietnam. That is the way it was, on December twenty-third, nineteen hundred and sixty-two. Good night and thank you for watching."

"What's a Vietnam?" Danny wondered aloud as he attached the caboose to the tanker car.

"It's a country," replied Rory, tightening the wires that connected the track to the transformer.

"You don't think there is going to be a war, do you, Dad?" asked Rory. Liam began matriculating for his degree in war at the age of eighteen. A management major, who learned to manage the unmanageable by convincing himself that the mangled Marine corpses, his fraternity brothers, were not human beings, but grotesque mannequins intended to scare people, like those in the spook house ride at Palisades Amusement Park. He took an elective in art; like his daughter, Liam's pencils had names too. Brain Grey. Liver Brown. Spleen Purple.

When Rory looked to his father for an answer, he could see that he had dozed off. Liam had missed the news. Rory did not want to disturb his father, and so the question about a war went unanswered.

15

CHRISTMAS EVE, 11:00 A.M.
SERENITY HOUSE.

Nora climbed the subway stairs and arrived on the sidewalk surrounded by a cadre of commuters. She checked her watch again as she continued the slow march on the snowy trail, trapped behind an elderly woman plodding in front of her, fully dependent on her cane. When finally freed of the geriatric obstacle, Nora rushed through a park where workers labored through the night clearing the snow, allowing hotdog venders to raise their blue-and-yellow umbrellas and disheveled chestnut roasters to ignite their charcoal ovens, laying a smokescreen that filled the air with the spirit of Christmas.

Father Horan knew that Nora and Shannon would eventually return home together when he left his note under the Downey door on Chauncey Street. Nora was familiar with the block the priest provided, but not the exact address. She remembered a tree-lined street with neglected brownstone buildings. A candy store sat next to an Italian deli and across the street from a pizzeria owned by two Greek brothers. There was no church on the street, Nora was certain of that. She was surprised that Father Horan had not called her to his office at Assumption of the Blessed Virgin Church, where Ernie broke his well-intentioned pledges and listened to sermons concerning the importance of family values.

The sidewalk in front of the buildings remained snow covered forcing Nora's retreat to the plowed road. She lumbered along on the slush-covered roadway, checking the house numbers. She paused in front of number thirty-five, where a shingle read, Serenity House.

Nora let the brass knocker mounted on the door drop from her hand. "Mrs. Downey?" A frail bag of bones appeared. Had Nora sneezed, he would have fallen over.

"Yes," replied Nora, gazing past him into the dimly lit foyer.

"My name is Peter. Welcome to Serenity House. Father Horan is waiting." His voice sounded as weak as he looked.

The residents of Serenity House wore clean shirts and ironed pants that fit the men who donated the garments but drooped on their new recipients, creating an armada of sagging sails waiting for a breeze. The denizens of the three-story brownstone busied themselves with housekeeping chores and added special attention to the oak staircase that emitted a sorrowful croak when tread upon. Two large rooms flanked the center hall. One served as a library and the other as a dining room, home to a large coffee urn suitable for an army mess hall that filled the first floor with a whiff of coffee and kept the cup each man held half-full. A sign on the dining room table warned: No smoking. Smoking causes fires. Smoke outside.

The fifty-year-old clergyman had no need for the banister when he came down the stairs. Father Horan was the spriest clergyman in the Archdiocese of Brooklyn. The crew of Serenity House, acknowledged their captain, displaying respect by pushing their mops and brooms with increased authority.

"Excuse me Mr. O'Brien. Is that a broom or a dance partner?" Father Horan asked.

"It's a broom, Father," replied O'Brien.

"You had me wondering there for a second." The priest turned toward another resident worker, who held a rag in his hand.

"And what are you laughing at Mr. Avanti?"

"Nothing Father."

"Nothing Father? Well, we cannot have that - can we Mr. Avanti?"

"No, Father," said the man meekly.

"Grab a shovel and start clearing a path. There are lots of old folk living on this block stranded by the snow," said Father Horan, administering an encouraging pat on the Avanti's shoulder.

"Right away, Father," said the man as he hurried out the door.

A maple tree, with branches that formed a leafy archway over the sidewalk in the summertime and, was older than the oldest brownstone on the street and blocked the view from Father Horan's office. The first true sunshine in days arrived unexpectedly and reflected off the snow-laden boughs, infiltrating the office with a brazen light.

"Thank you for coming Nora," said Father Horan extending his hand.

Nora eased into a clean but frayed sofa, like the furniture in the thrift store she shopped. The priest sat facing Nora, separated from her by a coffee table with a box of tissues and a glass ashtray. Father Horan removed a smoke from his black suit jacket.

"Breaking the rules aren't you, Father?" she asked rather brazenly.

"Rank has its privilege," he said with a smile lighting his smoke.

"Okay if I join you?" Nora began to dig in her pocketbook.

"Please," he said sliding the ashtray closer to Nora.

Horan had the cigarette lit as soon as it touched her lips. She exhaled a flume of smoke and scanned the room. A cross, made from shattered beer bottle glass hung over the door next to a portrait of Jesus Christ. Grey file cabinets lined one wall, atop of the cabinets was a garden of plastic plants in need of a dusting. Father Horan's oversized brown leather chair had aged into a relic that clung to the clergyman's form when he stood and embraced him like an old friend when he returned. His collection of books framed the office; sitting on his mahogany desk was a team of gifted doodads from past residents. Their significance, like their confessions, remained secret.

Nora had kept her promise to Liam and neatly brushed her hair and applied a hint of makeup. She had purchased a presentable coat at the Salvation Army with money borrowed from her brother and an almost new coat for Shannon, which she planned on wrapping as a present, after she attached the price tag she had removed from a coat in Alexanders Department store on Fordham Road. She vowed that next year Shannon would pick out a genuine new coat. Her fingernails, chewed to stubs, did not surprise Father Horan. He understood that the disease that consumed her husband had metastasized, the way it always did: destruction of the family, financial ruin, and ultimately death.

"Nice place you have here, Father," said Nora.

"It was donated many years ago and the cardinal converted it into Serenity House. I work here three days a week."

"So, everyone here . . . is a drunk?" she asked.

"Yes," Father Horan paused reflectively and took two short hits on his cigarette. "Yes, Nora, all drunks here."

"Good place for my husband then," she said leaning back into the sofa. "What is it they say Father? Misery loves company. But you know what I think Father?" A deep drag consumed half her smoke. "They don't look so miserable to me. I think they were freezing their balls off and that's why they are here. Listen to me, some way to talk to a priest."

"You can speak to me anyway you want," said the priest, assuming his role as whipping board.

She pushed the box of tissues aside and crushed out her cigarette. Nora made pledges too, just like Ernie. She would not need the tissues because she was not about to start bawling her eyes out as she had in the past.

"So why am I here Father?" she asked curtly.

"Because I asked you to come."

"Father Horan," Nora continued absent a trace of geniality, "I really don't have time for this."

"That's why you are here," explained Father Horan, "because I asked you to come and you came. You didn't have to."

"Okay. I'm here at Serenity House. The Hall of Fame for drunks. Now, the sixty-four-thousand-dollar question. Where is Ernie Downey?" she asked.

"He's here," Father Horan said.

"Where did you find him?" Nora had had enough of her husband.

"I didn't; he came on his own." The priest stood and walked to his desk, "after he got out of the holding pen in the Five-Two."

"I'm surprised he didn't call my brother."

"He did," he said, settling in his chair.

"Liam didn't tell me." Nora felt more disappointed than betrayed.

"He wanted him to know where he was, in case of an emergency. He asked your brother not to say anything. Ernie wanted to stay here but did not know if he could go the required seven days without a drink."

"What a laugh," Nora nervously crossed her legs, "Please tell me he did not say that. Because he is the emergency!"

"He hasn't had a drink in ten days." Horan's chair creaked as he shifted his weight.

"Wow. I think that might be some kind of Ernie Downey record." Nora's words were absent any attempt at civility. "Do you mind if I call his daughter?" she said, jokingly.

The sun that had brightened the room faded, leaving the priest in a dark shadow behind his desk.

"What a Christmas present!" Nora ranted on. "Better still, let me call the landlord. He will be thrilled. Maybe he will stop the eviction proceeding. What do you think of that, Father Horan?"

"He already has," he said, turning on the brass lamp on his desk. "I met him at Land Lord Tennant Court; he accepted a month's rent from me. The balance can be added monthly when Ernie gets back to work."

"Why would he do that?" she asked, surprised.

"Because I asked him to, and if Ernie doesn't pay, I will."

"He has no job," Nora stood, looked out the window, and watched Avanti, busy shoveling.

"He can have his job back when he returns from rehab, in thirty days."

"I don't understand why they would give him his job back." Nora turned toward the priest. "Let me guess, you asked them to."

"The union stepped in," he replied, adding, "He was a good electrician. Your husband is not the first member they helped and he will not be the last." Father Horan stood up and walked around the desk to Nora. "I have arranged for him to leave tomorrow. He would like to speak with you before he goes."

"I don't want to talk to him," she said, looking down at his desk.

"I didn't ask you to."

"No, you didn't."

"Nora, I'm not going to ask you to do anything, because you have done all you can."

"Thank you, Father," she whispered.

"Ernie has a letter for Shannon. He's waiting down the hall. If you want to take it to Shannon that would be fine. If not, I understand," said the priest.

■ ■ ■

Standing in the hall Ernie resembled a discarded wood dresser halfway through restoration. His was a face clinging to its last coat of varnish, sanded of its luster, and his eyes were set in an empty stare, aping the gaping holes from its missing drawers. A boy's shirt, with a grinning cowboy topped by a ten-gallon hat embroidered on the pocket, covered his skeletal frame.

The ghostly image standing in front of Nora exorcised the rage that consumed her and extinguished the roaring flames fed by the punishment she waited to inflict upon him. Suddenly, he no longer mattered. There was nothing left to hate; an alcohol-ravaged corpse looking for its sepulcher was all that remained of Ernie Downey.

Nora descended the stairs of Serenity House and stood beneath the ancient maple tree. She looked up, distracted by the sound of a pigeon furiously flapping its wings, unable to land on a snow-burdened branch. She stuffed the envelope Ernie had given her into her pocket and watched as the bird flew toward Court Street, where the subway back to Shannon waited.

16

A SNEAK PREVIEW ON HIGH HEELS.

Sky King landed safely. Fury was home, trotting around in his corral, and Jon Gnagy was ready to begin his TV class. Shannon assigned Danny the task of handing her Kate's pencils, which she had arranged in a tight numerical formation on the floor.

Kate looked up from her law dictionary; she was up to letter S, as in s*alus populi suprema lex: the welfare of the people is supreme law.* As she anticipated, the artist's tutorial was a repeat of the Christmas themed landscape that had aired the past three years, that frustrating rustic log cabin, pencils ten, twenty-four and thirty-three. Those puffs of smoke from the stone chimney, pencil eight. Nestled in the forest of pine trees, pencils six and fifteen. There was life in the landscape, with a father and son pulling a tree on a sled. Pencil thirty and forty-one.

Kate slipped out of the living room as soon as the class began. She dashed up the stairs and quickly knocked out their contrived code, three quick knocks delivered twice. Kate heard Mary blowing her nose as she approached a door decorated with a glittering Styrofoam reindeer and a Straw Spider web spun with black thread, waiting to trap a wish.

The Garvey apartment's décor was traditional Washington Heights, a three-cushion sofa and two chairs sealed in plastic that insulated the flowery fabric from the gooey drippings of peanut butter and jelly sandwiches.

A blonde wood cabinet, with black hinged doors, housed a TV with five ominous dials that only Mr. Garvey had a license to operate.

White linen curtains hung on the French doors, and, like in the Dunn apartment guarded a bed and dresser. Atop the dresser stood another wedding portrait. This groom, in his army uniform, with a blue and silver Combat Infantry Badge crowning two rows of campaign ribbons, posed with his solemn-looking bride.

Private First-Class Paul Garvey kept his part of the deal he had negotiated at oh - eight hundred hours on June 6, 1944, when he reintroduced himself to the Lord, while pinned down on Omaha Beach. He kept his promise and attended Mass every Sunday with his family and became a valued customer of Carmelo Costello, who sold him two Christ portraits, a Last Supper lithograph, and five identical crucifixes, one for each room.

Garvey was a card-carrying union man and a proud Democrat, made prouder by the election of the Irish Catholic Jack Kennedy whose portrait completed the Holy Trinity over the kitchen door. Kennedy next to Christ next to Franklin Roosevelt. The three icons, attached to walls throughout Washington Heights, were welcome guests at mealtimes.

The Garvey's were loyal Pedro customers and their tree stood in the same place as The Tree in the Dunn apartment. Mrs. Garvey swaddled her tree in angel hair, entombing the balsam fir in a white haze, like sea mist, thicker than fog, that subdued the glow of the lights.

Janet Garvey greeted people with a yawn in place of hello. She was an unhappy woman, who shared her unhappiness with her family three times a year. At Christmastime, it was the shopping the cooking and the constant sweeping of needles shedding from the tree and addressing all those Christmas cards and licking horrid-tasting two cent postage stamps. On Easter, the smell of boiling eggs became the villain. On the Fourth of July, the cherry bombs frightened her and the sparklers annoyed her. Her unhappiness became an occupation and she dedicated herself to being successful at it. The dire expression pasted on her face was like a sad clown mask that remained frozen in a weepy frown.

It was polite and proper for Kate to stop in the Garvey kitchen. Mary made the same cameo appearance on the way to Kate's room.

"Hello Mr. Garvey," said Kate.

Years of loading and unloading boxes kept Mary's father in a constant search for a position to ease the torturous back pain he mutely endured. He rarely ventured from the kitchen where the wooden table served not only meals, but also allowed Garvey to push himself up and out of a chair.

He was the sponsor of his daughter's red hair, and like Mary, his hair rejected a comb and sprung defiantly into the atmosphere in any direction it desired. Attached to his wrists were catcher's- mitt-size calloused hands that pulled stubborn steering wheels through miles of creeping city traffic.

"Hello, Missy." Mary pleaded with her father to drop the Missy moniker he attached to every female under the age of twenty – one. He was trying; the day before, he had only called his daughter Missy twice. He called her mother Mrs. Garvey instead of Janet, which drove Mary insane.

"Kate, Dad. Kate, Kate, Kate," instructed Mary.

"I'm sorry. How are you Kate?" he said apologetically.

Mr. Garvey liked Kate and appreciated the tutoring she provided that raised Mary's math grade from a C to a B + and got her accepted to The Sacred Heart of Mary Academy.

"Good, Mr. Garvey and how about this snow?" asked Kate politely.

"I was just telling Mrs. Garvey," Mary held her breath and turned brick red as he spoke, "that no one saw this coming, not even old Uncle Weatherbee."

Mary's brother Andy's four-year enlistment in the navy added to Janet Garvey's Christmas gloom. Andy had wanted nothing to do with the army, which was about to draft him for two years, and in which he had no inclination to serve. There was a time when she thought her son might be interested in the priesthood, which would have eliminated his problem with the draft board.

Andy enjoyed being an altar boy and did not protest when the time arrived for him to attend his confirmation classes. He did poorly in math but excelled in Latin. She thought that might be some sort of divine message. Then she discovered, hidden in his hockey bag, a year's worth of *Playboy* magazines, not the reading material one would expect from a future priest.

Jimmy the Jerk increased her Yule misery when she stopped in Stan's Candy Store to get a pack of cigarettes. He proclaimed with a protracted shaking, that a virtue of naval service was, "ya die clean, with a full stomach."

"Well, before you know it, you girls will be going to get your uniforms," said Mr. Garvey.

"It is seven months away, Paul." Mrs. Garvey's words, like her face were emotionless.

■ ■ ■

Mary performed her dance steps in rhythmic callisthenic like movements, an organized hopping about, performed to Twist and Shout playing on the hi-fi record player, a gift for her thirteenth birthday in November. She lost interest in dancing and collapsed on her bed, holding a photograph of Ricky Nelson. "I was wondering Kate, if I wrote to Ricky, now that we are official members of his fan club, do you think he would go with me to the Snowball?" Her words were more of a plea than a question.

Every girl who applied to SHM, had seen the picture in the school brochure of the Snowball Queen in her white gown. Each grade had its own Snowball dance, including the freshman class of 1963 that Kate and Mary would join.

"Of course, he would," said Kate while sorting through a stack of forty-five RPM records. "Gee whiz, you're on a first-name basis now."

"Stop being sarcastic," Mary held the photo close to her heart, "because I happen to be serious."

She rolled over on her side. "Sometimes they do stuff like that. Remember that dream date contest the girl won on American Bandstand with Dion?"

"Yes, I do remember," Kate said.

Kate started putting Mary's records in alphabetical order by artist name. "She was the girl who was always on the screen. I bet her father was the cameraman or a friend of Dick Clark. Fixed, that is what it was, all fixed. I'm still so glad I did not waste my time entering that stupid contest."

"You did. I entered us both," said Mary, speaking more to Ricky's picture.

"You what!" exploded Kate.

"I entered us in the contest," replied Mary.

"You had to be sixteen to enter the contest, Mary. I read the rules; they were very clear!"

"I guess I lied," said Mary fluffing her pillows.

"You submitted a fraudulent application. Do you know that's a crime?" Kate riled on.

"I already confessed. Three Hail Mary's, a Lord's Prayer, and Father Mooney said wait until I am sixteen to re- enter. It's over, Kate, no harm done. And stop gritting your teeth."

"But think of what might have happened," said Kate, turning her attention back to the records.

"Kate, you have to put that law dictionary down and please stop watching "The Defendants." It's making you nuts. Besides, neither one of us won; nothing happened."

"You should have asked me before you did such a thing."

"Why would I do that?" said Mary, putting Ricky's photo under her pillow. "You would have told me not to enter us," she said confidently.

"Please Mary, don't do stuff like that. You could ruin your life – our lives."

"You're waiting for that shoe to drop Kate. It's happening again, oh, yes, it is!" Mary mocked.

"What if it got in the newspaper?"

"You don't really think that - the newspapers!" said Mary, pretending to faint.

"I can see it on the front-page of the *Evening Post* – 'Girl lies to Dick Clark.' How would you explain that when it comes time to apply for college?"

"College?" said Mary half-joking. "I'm not going to college. I'm going to secretarial school; with a little luck, maybe we could sit next to each other."

"You didn't think you were going to SHM, but you're going," Kate sat on the bed next to Mary. "We are going to SHM and then we are going to Marymount College."

"You really believe that, don't you Kate?"

"I do. I want you to believe it too."

Kate stopped sorting through the records. "I think it's time to take Bobby down."

"Really? - it has only been two weeks." said Mary.

"It's been twenty-five days," Kate said correcting Mary.

"If we wait a week it will be a month. Let's wait."

"I think something might be happening and I need to find out now."

Mary closed her bedroom door and sanctimoniously removed a life size-poster of Bobby Darin from the door and placed it on her bed, next to Gypsy, Mary's rag doll and a companion since birth.

Two pencil marks on the door, separated by an eighth of an inch, dated weeks apart, glared at Kate. Mary grabbed her ruler from a desk cluttered with rolls of Christmas wrapping paper and a bag of ribbons and bows.

"I am starting to get a good feeling. I thought I noticed something but I didn't want to say anything," said Mary, waving the ruler in the air.

"Really?" Kate turned and placed her back against the door.

Mary stepped away and assessed Kate's posture. "Come on Kate, shoulders back, and head up."

"No cheating Mary," warned Kate, "I know you would. But please don't. Not even a sixteenth of an inch."

"I wouldn't," Mary promised.

"You would."

"I won't."

"You've done it before," Kate annoyingly reminded her friend.

"Well, not now."

"Well don't."

"Stop it already, or I'm not going to do it!"

Mary placed the ruler on Kate's head. It lined up perfectly with the mark made when they returned from the Macy's Thanksgiving Day parade.

"I knew it," Mary turned on her upbeat voice.

"What? And you better not be making it up."

"See for yourself." Mary made her mark on top of the ruler, not next to it, an early Christmas present of a full eighth of an inch.

"I was praying for a quarter of an inch. Did I tell you Rory and Danny are measuring each other?" Kate asked.

"No, you didn't."

"Danny has grown almost two inches this year," said Kate, sounding dejected.

"How about Rory?" asked Mary. Information concerning Rory Dunn was always welcome.

"It's obvious that Rory does not have height issues, Mary," said Kate studying the new mark on the door.

"No; I mean, now that you mention it, I guess not," replied Mary, more to herself.

"Two inches, that's normal. I saw the marks inside their closet. It has been going on since my mother put an end to Measurement Day. They don't think I know, but I do," announced Kate.

"Two inches. That's normal?" asked Mary rather skeptically.

"You didn't know that?" replied a shocked Kate.

"No, sorry Miss Know It All, I didn't."

"I can't believe you don't know that. Normal growth is two inches a year up to age fourteen."

"Well la - de - dah, isn't that good news you have two years of growing time left."

"Don't you see, Mary? Even if I grew another two inches I wouldn't be five feet tall. I can't even think about it. I am totally freaking out. I'll be writing four-eleven for the rest of my life."

"I'm sure it will happen," reassured Mary.

"You should know right now," said Kate, standing up on the bed, "I am not going to the Snowball."

"Please don't say that," said a dejected Mary.

"You can just forget about it. It is not going to happen," said Kate angrily adding, "I will look like some cartoon character, Mini Mouse comes to mind."

"I agree, Kate; you would look like a cartoon character," Mary placed the ruler back on her desk.

"Oh, thank you, Mary Garvey, what a friend. Exactly what I needed to hear," lamented Kate.

"Cinderella is what comes to my mind. I wish I looked like you Kate. Look at this hair. Let me ask you, Kate. What do you think my hair will look like in two years! Someone please tell me what I did to deserve this. You want to switch places Kate? Because I'm ready," said Mary.

"You? Look at me. I will need stilts, like a circus clown. Maybe Miss Grimes can lend me a pair."

"Guess what?" Mary whispered loudly.

"What?"

"We will be wearing stilts," said Mary with a devilish smile on her face, "and your practice pair are under the bed."

Mary removed two shoeboxes from under her bed. "I found these in the Lutheran Church thrift- shop."

Mary slipped on her pair of high heels, violet with a matching bow. She took two wobbly steps toward the window and then attempted to execute an about face, but her ankles collapsed like a first-time ice skater and she tumbled on to the bed.

"Early Christmas presents for both of us," said an upbeat Mary adding, "We've been good."

She paused and corrected herself. "Well, you've been good. Go ahead and give it a try."

Kate opened her box and examined the bright yellow shoes with the same menacing heel. She quickly put on the shoes and took three baby steps, thinking that would be easier, in the direction of the measuring door with her arms extended the way the two eight-year-old friends use to balance themselves when they used the sidewalk curb as a tightrope.

Kate slowly rotated, winding up with her back against the door. Mary kicked off the shoes and grabbed her ruler.

"I know it's cheating," said Kate.

"It's not cheating. It is a substitution until you grow the two inches. It's a sneak preview."

"Let me have the ruler, Mary." Kate spoke her words so quickly they were barely audible.

She measured from the floor to the new shoe-assisted mark on the door. "I'm five feet and one eighth of an inch."

"Merry Christmas, Kate."

"Merry Christmas to you, Mary."

"So," warned Mary with a smile, "no more talk of not going to the Snowball."

Mary placed Bobby back on her door, diligently realigning the thumb-tack holes. Kate could walk the length of the room with her arms at her side. Mary interpreted Kate's success as a challenge and quickly put on her shoes and set the window as her destination.

"Rory is crossing the street," said Mary looking out of the window, as if she had witnessed Moses crossing the Red Sea with the Egyptians in pursuit.

"He does that all by himself now Mary," joked Kate, improving with each step.

"He's not by himself. He's with that Frankie Romano from 172nd Street."

"Who?" asked Kate, balancing her way toward Mary.

"Frankie Romano, the quarterback that cute Italian guy," said Mary flatly.

"Oh? I wouldn't know." Kate kept Frankie thoughts to herself.

"Andy says they think he might be the best quarterback to ever play for All Hallows," said Mary continuing her practice walk. "Some people think he might even be good enough to play for Notre Dame. Next year, he will be starting varsity quarterback. That's what Andy says."

Without warning, tears began to flow down Mary's cheeks.

"Mary, what's wrong?" said Kate, kicking off the shoes.

Mary sat on the bed and picked up Gypsy, "I'm sorry, it just hits me sometimes. I am going to miss my brother. I miss him already and he hasn't even left yet. I don't know what I will do when he's gone. I hate it. I hate this whole damn military thing."

"He's going to be okay, Mary," Kate sat next to Mary. "Look at Teresa's brother Eddie. He went in the navy and wound up at the Brooklyn Navy Yard. He was home every other weekend," she said, trying to be upbeat.

"I guess that could happen," said Mary wiping away her tears.

"Sure, it could," added Kate while fighting the image of Andy floating face down in the water, one more shoe on her mental shelf waiting to drop.

Kate and Mary listened to records and worked on their Savoy dance steps barefoot after they tripped out of their high heels four times. Kate checked the time. Dinner at the Dunn house was always at six o'clock when Liam was home and Kate looked forward to the meals.

"Got to go Mary. I am taking Danny to see Santa tomorrow at Woolworth's. Want to go with us?" asked Kate.

"Sure, then we can go to Nedick's for a hotdog," replied Mary.

■ ■ ■

"I don't get it, Frankie," said Rory.

"I wish I could help you out, Rory."

Kate clung to her shoebox. She struggled to decipher the conversation, the words blurred within a chorus of "Oh Holy Night" that resounded from behind Joey Carlo's door on The Delicious Fourth. She descended three steps; the dialogue between the teammates grew louder but the meaning of their words remained unclear to Kate.

"Why would they need a lawyer?" asked Rory.

Lawyer, who needs a lawyer? thought Kate. The words Kate heard made her feel anxious; she sat down on the hallway steps.

"Maybe, and I'm just thinking out loud, maybe they had a will done." posed Frankie. "People do that all of the time. I heard my parents talking about it. And with your dad being a cop - oh wow, I'm sorry I said that Rory." He sounded more than sincere.

"That's okay, Frankie. I know what you meant. I just hope no one is in trouble. It would be great news if a will was what this is all about," said Rory.

"Did you mention anything to Kate?" asked Frankie.

Kate feasted on the sentence, shocked that Frankie knew that she even existed, but it did nothing to stop the eddy of fear she was swirling in. The shoes in her mind were lining up to drop. Sucked away were the happy thoughts of SHM, the high heel growth spurt, and the 1964 Snowball dance.

"No, I didn't want to ruin her Christmas. Something like this would make her nuts. But I do know this: Kate would not have left Brian Kelly's office without finding out what was in that envelope," said Rory.

"And you are sure that was the envelope."

"Oh yeah. It had Danny's stamp on it. It was the envelope all right."

Kate could visualize the envelope on the kitchen table, the one her mom said contained a plan for a new shade. The one Danny put his Santa stamp on. The big vanilla envelope that required a mouthful of saliva to seal and a contrived response from her mom when asked about its content. *That envelope,* thought Kate.

She had heard enough. She decided to alert the football players to her presence and so she dropped her shoebox, which unexpectedly sent one shoe down the stairs toe over heel as if it were Danny's Slinky.

The boys turned their attention up the stairwell. Kate picked up her shoe. She felt small again with her stilts back in their box under her arm. She stopped on the third step above the landing, which made her taller than Rory and placed his teammate closer than he had ever been to Kate.

"Hi, Kate," said Rory.

Kate felt awkward in her silence.

"You know Frankie. Frankie Romano," said Rory unlocking the door.

"Yes." Kate paused, adding softly, "the quarterback."

Frankie lived five blocks away, as distant as the stars in Washington Heights, where a street called "my block" was like a sovereign nation, as unique as a set of fingerprints. A block he shared with a cast of characters he knew his entire life. A block with its own egg cream factory candy store and a regiment of stickball players who played by their own strictly enforced ground rules.

Frankie was taller, broader, and older looking than her brother with a persona befitting the leader of a football team. A Romanesque nose dominated his face and fit perfectly between his chiseled cheekbones. His hair, as black as wet asphalt matched his eyes. In the summer, Kate would glance over the top of a book in his direction at Highbridge swimming pool, where his Mediterranean skin browned like a pizza crust and was on full display.

Kate was certain he drew the attention of the girls who watched from marble stoops when he drove a Spalding three sewers with a broomstick and then sprinted around bases, drawn with Indian chalk, like a thoroughbred racehorse.

When the Dunn family went to cheer on Rory and his team, Kate would discretely observe the star quarterback from the stands, occasionally borrowing her dad's binoculars for a closer look, which Colleen kindly ignored. Unfortunately, for Kate, Brother Anthony kept Frankie's face hidden in his helmet even when he was on the sideline; he ran his team that way. Everyone was ready from the time the national anthem played until the clock ticked down. No one sat on the bench, and no one would dare take a knee.

Kate and Danny passed Frankie most mornings, on opposite sides of the street when she and her little brother were on their way to Incarnation, and he was walking for the bus to All Hallows. Her game plan was ready for execution after Christmas; she would walk on the same sidewalk as Frankie. Kate discovered that her day went better, when it began with a look at Frankie Romano.

Mary, thought Kate, *can have Ricky Nelson*. She would figure out a way to have the senior from All Hallows, be her date to the sophomore Snowball dance, she hoped by then to be five feet one inch without stilts.

Kate surmised that Rory invited Frankie over to their apartment to study the mimeographed playbook filled with mysterious X's and O's that her brother studied the way she studied her law dictionary. All Hallows was playing Cardinal Hayes for the junior varsity championship game on

Randalls Island after Christmas break. Rory reported that the starting half back had injured his knee, so he would be playing both halfback and middle linebacker.

"Cardinal Hayes has one darn good defense," said Liam, hanging Shannon's Christmas landscape on the wall behind the kitchen table, the artwork modified by Shannon to a father and daughter pulling the sled. Danny loved the interesting twist Shannon had created in the landscape by sketching an angel in the chimney smoke. She had drawn it in such a way that it needed to be pointed out, a detail which added to its mystique.

"Some hit you took against Spellman. How does that shoulder feel now Frankie?" asked Liam.

"Good Mr. Dunn, ready to go," replied Frankie, following Rory to his room.

■ ■ ■

Frankie departed for 172nd Street with his playbook under his arm and Liam's mind at ease with the knowledge that the quarterback would be ready to play in the biggest game of the year. Shannon and Danny settled in on the couch watching *It's a Wonderful Life,* her favorite Christmas movie.

Kate closed her door and slowly walked to her window. She watched Frankie cross Wadsworth Avenue; her eyes remaining fixed on him until he turned the corner and vanished from her sight. She sat at the vanity and removed her favorite Jack Kennedy campaign button from the mirror, the big one that read, "Win With Jack." She slowly turned it in her hand and returned to contemplating the envelope sitting in Brian Kelly's law office. She agreed with Frankie: it might be a will.

A disturbing scene revisited her: Liam stuffing the turkey before they left for the Thanksgiving Day Parade. Danny asking their father for the ten thousandth time, "Can we get a dog, Dad?" Instead of the usual quick refusal of the request that came with a host of reasons why a dog does not belong in an apartment, a different conversation ensued.

"And what would you name a dog Danny?" asked Liam smiling at Colleen.

"Lassie, I would name it Lassie."

"What if it's a boy dog Danny?" queried Rory.

"I would still name him Lassie. Lassie is the best name for a dog, any dog. Right Kate."

"Lassie would be good Danny," said Kate.

A solid rap on the door startled Kate. She knew it was Rory; he never barged in like her little brother and the knock always arrived the same way, two quick hits, delivered with his knuckle.

"Come in," said Kate softly.

Rory stood silently looking at his sister before he spoke. "You heard me and Frankie talking in the hall."

"Not everything," said Kate putting the campaign button back in its place.

Rory closed the door. "You heard enough."

"Something about a lawyer," replied Kate.

"When I went back to Kelly's office to get paid I saw the envelope on the desk. So much for mom's lampshade story," said Rory sarcastically.

"Tomorrow we will find out what this is about."

"I could just come out and ask Mom what the heck is going on."

"No, leave it with me. After I take Danny to see Santa I will stop at Kelly's office."

"Okay. I am sure this is all about nothing. If you want I could go with you."

"No, I'll be fine. Monica Broome is an easy lock to pick," said Kate, thinking about Lassie.

17

CHRISTMAS EVE
2:00 P.M.
HOTDOGS AND LOCK PICKING.

A woman cashier disguised as an elf, handed Danny a balloon with a Santa face that looked like a police mug shot. It became obvious to Kate that the yawning Santa, who impatiently listened to the wishes of children since the day after Thanksgiving, yearned to return to his custodial duties. Danny declined the not so jolly old elf's invitation to sit on his knee. He stared skeptically at the skinny Santa, whose oily black hair slid from under a silly cotton wig. Danny did his best to avoid the Santa imitator's face, which was hidden behind a bogus beard with tobacco stains around the lips.

The abrupt conversation between Danny and Santa saddened Kate. Her little brother was growing up, causing Kate to struggle with the thought that 1962 might be the last Christmas Danny would ask her about the magic key that opened all doors.

Shannon sculptured the sauerkraut, relish, and onions that covered her hotdog into a culinary Christmas tree that caught everyone in Nedick's attention. Kate watched her cousin's diligent fingers turn the wrapper from her straw into a star, which she placed on top of the tree. Danny became a calligrapher, his quill a tube of mustard and neatly inscribed his name on a hotdog. A giant swig of the orange drink he savored followed each bite and puffed up his red cheeks like a gerbil's. Mary feasted on an order of French fries, whitened from the blizzard of salt she happily applied, and then matched Danny gulp for gulp of the addictive drink. But the thought of the pending meeting with Monica Broome had stolen Kate's appetite. She slowly slid the remaining half of her hotdog across her plate concealing it under her napkin and checked her watch. She was ten minutes ahead of the schedule she had fabricated during a restless night.

■ ■ ■

Danny injected a skip to his steps, to keep up with his sister. The goggles on the Johnnie Blast flying helmet hid half of his face and brought smiles to all of those he passed. He held out Dart and navigated the plane around Washington Heights' shoppers with their arms chock-full with bags of holiday groceries or that special last-minute gift.

The light on the corner of 177th Street and Saint Nicholas Avenue began to turn red. Kate could have easily crossed the street safely, but she believed light beating sent a bad message to Danny and so she held her little brother's hand tightly and waited for a car to pass slowly by.

"What's wrong Kate?" asked Mary, getting ready to blow her nose.

"Nothing," replied Kate with her eyes stoically focused straight ahead.

"It's Christmas Eve; you haven't spoken two words all day. I hope this isn't about that stupid contest."

"It's not. I'm fine," said Kate faking an upbeat reply.

"Something to do with Frankie Romano?"

"I like Frankie," interrupted Danny loudly, "He's the best quarterback, and Rory is the best linebacker."

"Why would I be the least bit concerned with Frankie Romano?" said Kate, looking up at Mary and trying to control herself.

"I don't know," said Mary placing her tissue back in her pocket, "I was just thinking..."

Kate pounced on Mary's words. "Don't think too much Mary; it's never a good idea." She instantly regretted her reaction.

"I'm sorry Mary. I didn't mean that." The last thing she needed was a fight with her friend.

"Yes, you did. When a person is as smart as the great Kate Dunn they mean everything, they say," said Mary plaintively.

The light turned green, but no one moved. Mary knelt in front of Danny and lifted the goggles from his eyes, placing them on top of his head. "Danny, I have to go and get a present for my mom. I want you to have a merry Christmas, okay?"

"Okay," said Danny looking at the ground.

"Mary . . . I'll see you tonight, for midnight Mass," said Kate but Mary ignored her.

"I'll see ya around Shannon," said Mary, walking away.

"I hope so," replied Shannon.

"Mary!" Kate's voice added fuel to Mary's steps, sending her briskly back toward 181st Street.

"Shannon! Watch Danny and do not cross the street. Wait right here!" ordered Kate.

"Mary!" Kate called out before she caught up with her friend. "Mary, please listen to me, you're my best friend."

Mary stopped but refused to turn around. "I'm your only friend."

"Something is going on Mary, and I should have told you."

"It is Frankie. I was right."

"I wish. I wish that were it, Mary." Her words sounded as if she were rubbing a genie's lamp.

"Then what is it?" Mary looked over her shoulder and became concerned. "What's going on Kate?"

"I'm not sure. Not yet, anyway."

"I think a hint would be nice."

"Brian Kelly," Kate replied with words as cold as The Freeze.

"The lawyer?" asked a befuddled Mary.

"Right. Rory found out that my parents have something going on with him, and it is very upsetting. So, I'm sorry for what I said. I didn't mean it."

"Okay let's forget about it. What do you want me to do?" asked Mary.

"I hope there will be nothing for any of us to do, but I'll let you know later."

■ ■ ■

Kate knew the rule. Mike Hickey allowed the kids, many of whose parents were customers, to use the peanut machine in the vestibule of the High Spot Bar, which dispensed the saltiest peanuts in all of New York City. But entrance to the bar remained forbidden.

Kate had four cents ready, enough to purchase a palm load for Danny and Shannon. Danny loved twisting the pennies in the machine and holding out his hand. Once he devoured the peanuts, he lapped at his palm like a frisky puppy.

The door to the bar was ajar. Shannon was familiar with the recipe of the air seeping out of the High Spot, a cauldron of smoldering cigarettes that mixed with the silt from the river of beer that flowed from high-handle taps, backed up with a shot of whiskey. It was the same odor that hung on her father's clothes like cheap after-shave on the few nights he returned to Chauncey Street.

Kate's watch read two o'clock. She knew Kelly's schedule because Kate observed him walking across 177th Street and into the High Spot Bar every day during the summer at exactly two o'clock. She made the same observations during Christmas and Easter breaks from Incarnation. Kate looked into the darkened bar as Danny toyed with the wheel on the peanut machine. Brian Kelly sat where he always sat, at the end of the bar beneath the television mounted on the wall.

Luckily for Kate, Danny was anxious to get home. *Miracle on Thirty Fourth Street* was coming on "Million Dollar Movie," and Shannon wanted to return to a picture she was working on for a Christmas present no one had seen because she worked on it in the bathroom.

"You guys go home. I have to pick up something for Mom," said Kate.

Kate stood in front of the High Spot and watched her little brother and cousin race back to 650 and scamper up the steps. She crossed the street passing Jimmy the Jerk who was leaving Stan's Candy Store with a brown bag tucked under his arm. He paused every ten steps, allowing an unseen lightning bolt to jolt his body.

■ ■ ■

Kate slipped into the law office undetected. She had memorized the picture Rory insisted on drawing, so she would know exactly where the envelope would be. She peeked around Monica's door and eyed the leafy potato vine, but the envelope was not there. It was nowhere to be seen on the desk cluttered with file folders and unopened mail. She watched as Monica Broome discarded her blindfold and typed with both hands on the home keys with her face fixed on the *Learn to Type* book. Her accuracy was improving, but her speed remained at a frustrating twenty words per minute.

"Hi Monica," said Kate stepping in front of Brian Kelly's assistant.

Monica and Kate were city neighbors; they lived in the same building, and subjected to a protocol for communal living that dictated that a proper distance exist between them. Cordial chats remained limited to a pleasant hello and good-bye, because apartment dwellers guarded each other's privacy religiously.

Monica looked up and reached for her cigarettes. Like everyone else in 650, she was aware of Kate's academic achievements. She called Kate, "The Brain" and was still upset with Brian Kelly after he hinted that Kate might be helpful during the summer, just a few hours a day.

Monica had nothing to fear from The Brain. What she knew concerning the Dunn family allowed her to project a sly smile even though Monica's boss forbid her from sharing the information she possessed. "We don't want anyone to know about this." That is what the client, who was also a New York City cop said.

"Hello Kate." Monica eyed Kate deviously, as she lit her cigarette. "What's up?"

"I just wanted to let Mr. Kelly know that I won't be able to work here in the summer."

No, you will not, thought Monica, as she exhaled a long and steady plume of smoke in Kate's direction. "Oh, really? I'm sorry to hear that." Playing dumb was easy for Monica. "I guess another offer came up."

"No, it's just that with what's going on... you know, being involved; you being a legal secretary. I want to be a legal secretary too," lied Kate.

Monica was no more a legal secretary than a mop pusher working in a hospital was a surgeon. She knew that, but Kate's words were nice to hear. "Well I'm sure you will be very good at it." Monica discretely slid a piece of paper over the typing textbook.

"My brothers and I are so excited," said Kate as dramatically as she could.

Monica studied the glowing ash forming on her cigarette. Apparently, Kate was aware of the matter her boss had completed that very morning. *No surprise,* reasoned Monica; it was exciting news for the Dunn family. The Brain had every reason to be happy.

"The paperwork was finished this morning," said Monica confidently while flipping an ash off her cigarette.

"Yes, my father said it would be. My mom delivered it last week and my silly little brother Danny, he put the Santa sticker on it." The fish was on the hook. Just a matter of reeling her in.

"Oh, that - that was the insurance policy Mr. Hooper got for your parents."

Kate wanted to hug Monica and grumpy old Mister Hooper. The words *insurance policy* could only mean one thing... a will. Frankie was right.

Kate could hardly wait to return home with the good news. What a wonderful Christmas present for Rory, and Lassie would remain on her farm with her young master, Jeff.

"They will need it for the closing. That's the day they sign all the papers," said a confident Monica.

Kate struggled to catch her breath. She loosened her scarf in a futile attempt to gain her composure.

"Yes, I guess you cannot do anything without the insurance policy," said Kate. Her fish, now a great white shark, was about to lock its jaws on Kate.

"I'm kinda' jealous of you Kate. But who knows . . . just between us girls, maybe one day, when Mr. Right comes along, I might have a house too. With a back yard and a picnic table, and maybe a little garden in front." Monica paused and adjusted the potato plant vine.

"Brian," Monica quickly corrected herself, "I mean Mr. Kelly, he says the banks are going to be getting really busy with all those homes being built out in that place Hicksville. Why would anyone name a place Hicksville? Who wants to be a hick anyway?"

Kate threw up the hot dog in the alley next to Tip Top Printing. She kept heaving in uncontrollable spasms, leaving only the bile from her stomach to regurgitate and form a yellow puddle on the snow under her feet. She spit out the last morsels of vomit from her mouth and ruined her white scarf when she swiped it across her lips.

18

Danny waited for the show to begin. He sat in the prized 'house seat' like he always did, on his bed, center orchestra: no obstructed view of the stage for Danny Dunn when his mom converted his room into a winter spectacular.

The frozen clothes Colleen pulled through the bedroom window off the squeaky clothesline that spanned the alley morphed into a menagerie of wonderful creatures. One of Rory's white school shirts became a swan; a pillowcase transformed into a rabbit. A sock became a mouse, and a pair of dungarees somehow became an elephant, posed with his trunk held high in the air.

"I don't see any angels yet, Danny," said Colleen looking out the open window while buttoning up her red cardigan sweater.

"Who do you see Mom?" asked Danny pulling on his Johnny Blast flying helmet.

"I'm not sure it's getting dark in the alley... wait just one minute. Why, look who it is!"

"It's Christmas Swan!" exclaimed Danny as he launched Dart on a short flight that ended at Shannon's feet when she entered the room.

"What swan?" asked a suspicious Shannon.

Colleen eased the frozen shirt into the room. The arms were stiff, with one locked in what looked like a wave. The shirt protested with a crunching sound as Collen spread its tails and then sat it on the floor where it stood on its own, at rigid attention.

Colleen had to work quickly, before Flann's steam heat took its toll on the frozen garment and sent it to the floor and becoming a cotton puddle. A bend, a tuck and a pull: suddenly, a white swan stood where the shirt had been, answering Shannon's question.

Danny and Shannon wrapped themselves in a blanket as The Freeze invaded the room. Colleen removed two clothespins from a pillowcase, placed them in the canvass bag that sat at the base of the window, and quickly created a rabbit with oversized ears that she could bend in half.

"I think," Colleen looked out of the window, her voice was full of anticipation, "I think yes, it's the Linen Angel."

"The Linen Angel is my favorite!" exclaimed Danny.

Frozen to perfection. Colleen sensed it as soon as she touched the sheet on the clothesline. Persuading it through the window required a firm but gentle touch, like raising a child. Colleen clung to the stiff sheet and took two steps backward. Then she returned to the window, removed two more clothespins, and again danced the sheet backward into the room.

A clothespin fell to the floor; Danny leaped from the bed and picked it up. There were so many wonderful things to do in Danny's Clothespin World, like painting faces on them and making them passengers on the Popsicle stick rafts he launched down the gutter on rainy summer days. Or he and his brother attaching them on their noses when they held their breaths and dunked their heads in the bathtub, competing in an endurance test that Danny always seemed to win.

The stiff sheet clung to the ancient window guard. Colleen tugged on the sheet, a test for the twenty-year-old wood screws. She looked like a surfcaster backing an exhausted blue fish up and on to the beach. Each yank on the sheet sent another clothespin into the canvass bag. Once the cotton iceberg was inside, Colleen set to work.

After several magical maneuvers, the Linen Angel's wings appeared. Then her head took form as Colleen gently guided it forward as if the angel were gazing down into the black alley. Her arms came together and the ends of the sheet became prayerful hands.

Danny suddenly thought of a new game to play with the clothespins. He was getting smarter; he kept the thought to himself. Rory might approve, but his parents certainly would not. He knew Kate would never allow his new game. He would play it later when he was alone in the room, after the angel crumpled to the floor.

19

Flann McFarland busied himself in the vestibule, replacing dead light bulbs and buffing the brass mailboxes. A polite bow and a smile greeted the tenants when they returned from running last minute holiday errands, with an especially warm greeting for those who slipped a Christmas envelope under his door. He hoped his last-minute efforts would serve as a reminder, for those who missed the opportunity to partake in the joy of Christmas giving.

Flann picked up his Pine-Sol- soaked mop that created a magic carpet ride that filled the halls with the fragrance of summertime, when his mop kept stickball players and key-tossing hopscotch hoppers trapped on the stoop waiting for the super's wet floors to dry.

He lugged the bucket up to the second-floor landing, struggling with each step, and placed it in front of Miss Grimes's door, decorated with Danny's artwork and a Straw Spider web. Flann slowly slung the mop across the tile floor. When he turned back to his bucket, Grimes was standing in her doorway.

White fur trimmed her sleeves and the hem of her green dress. Her turban was green too and matched her stockings, which drew attention to her red rubber boots. Flann thought she looked like an ornament for a

Christmas tree but kept that to himself, because sitting on the floor next to the dwarf was a shopping bag filled with what looked like multi- colored cotton candy billiard balls that he knew would be delicious. "Well, well, 'tis Miss H. Wellington Grimes herself and a merry Christmas Eve to ya." A holiday truce had come to exist between Flann and the snow-predicting tenant from apartment twenty-two. And with the sweet smell of cotton candy filling Flann's hallways he saw no reason not to be polite.

Grimes was not the only busy tenant. Preparations behind the doors of 650 were underway. Frozen turkeys bobbed and thawed in bathtubs filled with tepid water and once-fresh loafs of Silvercup bread, soon to be holiday stuffing, sat exposed to the air and turned crisp.

"I hope you did not hurt your back shoveling the snow, Flann," said Grimes with a chuckle while sorting through her bag of cotton candy under Flann's watchful eye.

"Not at all. Happy I am for the children and the adults too I might be addin'. I've never seen so many Straw Spider webs."

"And with my twine there will be even more webs." Grimes reached into the bag with her white gloved hand and removed a ball of red cotton candy. "Here you are Flann, Merry Christmas."

"And a fine web I will be spinning for my door. And ya never know, even an old man like myself might be havin' a wish granted."

Flann watched as Miss Grimes scurried up the stairs with her shopping bag filled with cotton candy twine. He could hear her knocking on the doors of the children of 650. Third floor Sean was her fist stop.

"Which color would you like Sean?" asked Grimes.

"Red! Red would make a nice web," replied Sean, staring at the shopping bag.

"I made extra balls of red. People seem to love red. Pick out the one you like."

Sean dug in the bag, removed a red ball of Grimes's cotton candy, and was surprised at the weight of it.

"Wow, how did this cotton candy get so heavy?" asked Sean as he tossed the ball in the air and caught it.

"I wove them especially for the Straw Spiders. You do believe in Straw Spiders?"

"Well, I am going to make a wish that's for sure. I haven't figured out what to wish for yet, but I will be making a wish."

20

The wind carried dark clouds that destroyed the starry, moonlit sky fore-casted by Uncle Weatherbee. Instead, a blustery dusk descended upon the streets and chased home the last procrastinating Christmas shoppers. The friendly mechanical spaceman stood alone and unplugged in Hobby Land's window, unable to wave hello or good-bye. His friend, the giant stuffed panda bear, and the toy soldiers who guarded him now hid in clos-ets, anxiously waiting to meet their new owners.

The proprietor of Hobby Land returned from the back of his store with the present Rory had been making payments on and placed it on the counter. The exhausted merchant, with barely a stocking stuffer left to sell and a family of his own to get home to patiently watched his last customer empty his pockets of crumpled-up dollar bills and then dash out of the door.

Rory tucked the present under his arm as if it were a football and walked hurriedly past junk yards of snow, gray heaps that cast unsavory shadows on the sidewalks. The beacon atop the George Washington Bridge sprang to life and swept the sky over him, sending the seagulls that perched within its stark steel frame diving toward the leafless forest beneath the bridge and home to their secluded nests.

A fierce gust collided with Rory on Broadway in front of the High Spot Bar, forcing him to stop and seek refuge in the vestibule. A customer stumbled out of the door, holding it open long enough for Rory to see Brian Kelly slumped over a shot of whiskey and Mitch Miller on the TV with a ball bouncing over the words of "White Christmas."

He followed the drunk out of the High Spot and raced across the street, bounding over mounds of snow, and avoiding the people who mustered together on the corner, waiting to traverse a narrow-shoveled ravine. Rory pressed his nose against the glass door at Kelly's law office. The fish tank cast a flickering eerie light that illuminated the troublesome envelope on Monica's desk. A hand grabbed Rory's shoulder. He spun around, ready to fight.

"You scared the hell out of me, Jimmy!" yelled Rory.

"I'm sorry. I wouldn't want to do that." Jimmy the Jerk began to have a shaking spasm but the whiskey Rory could smell on his breath kept it to five seconds.

"I saw Kate. She didn't look so good," said Jimmy.

"What do you mean?" Rory asked skeptically.

"She came out of Mr. Kelley's office and I said hello and she didn't say hello back, and she never acts like that. I hope I didn't do something wrong."

"I'm sure you didn't Jimmy," said Rory, walking away.

Rory was oblivious to the stellar light show emanating from the apartment windows on 177th Street. Even Miss Grimes' burlap bag windows were glowing with Christmas lights. Thoughts of his sister and her meeting with Monica Broome made all the joy and anticipation that was Christmas Eve in Washington Heights disappear.

The splendid-looking tree in the window of the garage next to 650 shone brightly too. It cast its light on the Stranger who stood at the top of the stairs leading to Flann's basement. The Stranger quickly turned away, but not before Rory caught a glimpse of his face. After three steps Rory stopped and looked again in his direction. The face looked familiar but, Rory could not be certain. He could not remember seeing Flann out of the uniform he wore every day: the khaki pants, and the brown boots he buffed but never polished. More surprising, the eternally present corncob pipe was not in his mouth or his hand.

"Flann?" said Rory, thinking more about what he would learn when he returned home. The Stranger pulled up the collar of his pea coat and walked slowly away, leaving Rory to wonder what was troubling the captain of 650.

21

Liam watched the cat clock, a Mother's Day gift from Rory, on the kitchen wall. The plastic feline annoyingly ticked with each swing of its black tail that served as a pendulum perfectly in sync with a set of rolling eyes. The cat's face read ten minutes past five. Kate's being ten minutes late would have been of no consequence to any other father. But Liam Dunn had never been and never would be like any other father.

Liam managed the demons of his past by orchestrating the present. When he returned from the war, he became a cop to protect people. He needed to do that, to make things right, to place himself between the innocent and those who would do them harm. He began to renegotiate the deal he had made with the Lord, to ensure there was no misunderstanding, as did the other deal makers did who survived the war, like his neighbor, Paul Garvey. But unlike Garvey, Liam would never be a customer of Carmelo's Religious Gift Shop or desecrate Incarnation Church with his presence. That wasn't part of his deal. He would descend into the grave where and when it pleased God, and he would report as ordered to hell. And the Lord would keep his part of the bargain and not seek retribution by taking his children as payment for the lives of the children hiding in the cave whom he had incinerated.

"I'm home," said Rory softly. He moved quickly to his room and prepared for the barrage of questions about Kate that he was certain would commence. His little brother sat beneath the window, engrossed with Dart and the clothespins strewn on the floor.

Rory looked up from his bed at his parents, who were standing in front of him. "Where's your sister?" Liam sternly asked.

"She went shopping," said the ever-helpful Danny while holding up Dart to admire the clothespin he had fastened over the cockpit of the glider.

"I didn't ask you Danny," snapped Liam. Aggravated, he flipped open his Zippo, lit a smoke, and took a deep drag.

"I don't know where she is. Like Danny said, I guess she went shopping." Liam processed the answer and concluded that it was not a lie but a cover story to protect Kate.

Rory knew his father wasn't buying any of it, but he wasn't giving up his sister. He knew where she had gone but had no idea where she was. What he knew was that her visit to Brian Kelly's law office didn't end the way they had hoped it would: with the discovery that a will was why his parents were dealing with Brian Kelly. If that were the case, Kate would have long since been home happily preparing for Christmas Eve in apartment thirty-one.

Liam swiftly determined that he'd harvested all the information he was going to get from his son and turned his attention to Colleen. "Call the Garvey's Colleen, and find out if Mary knows where Kate is." Liam went into full cop mode as the haunting screams of the children dragged him back to the cave on Tarawa and suffocated him in fear.

Visions of his daughter laying in some alley butchered, the sacrificial lamb for his own sin played out in front of him.

Colleen went to the phone while Liam went shopping for answers. He found his niece sitting on the floor in Kate's room, spinning a Straw Spider web from the contents of her aunt's sewing basket.

"Where did Kate say she was going?" asked Liam.

"Shopping," replied a leery Shannon.

"Shopping where?" probed Liam, hoping for an answer.

"She didn't say," answered Shannon, refusing to look away from the basket.

"And you didn't think of asking?"

Colleen entered the room, twisting a handkerchief in her hands. "I spoke with Mary; she doesn't know where Katherine is."

"Was Mary crying on the phone?" asked Liam. He masked his fears as he had since the day he became a father.

"No, she wasn't," responded Colleen failing in her attempt to sound calm.

Liam smothered her in his arms and whispered the words Colleen prayed to hear and he longed to deliver softly in her ear, words spoken when their lives suddenly went into a skid and Liam steered them safely back on to the road. "Listen to me, Colleen… we're good."

Liam led the way up the stairs oblivious to the sound of a Christmas carol from apartment thirty-four and the aroma of baking cookies from apartment forty-one. Liam would get the information he knew Mary had about his daughter. He had first met Mary in the park when he'd placed Kate in the swing next to her, when all they could say was goo-goo to each other. Mary knew where Kate was and what she was up to. And he also knew Kate wasn't Christmas shopping.

Colleen rang the doorbell. Liam grew inpatient and was about to rap on the door when Paul Garvey appeared, dressed for midnight Mass in his white shirt adorned with an epic tie that was wide enough to depict a mountain landscape populated with a heard of moose.

"Hello Liam, hi, Colleen," Mary's dad wasted no time in getting to the point. "What's going on with Kate?"

"That's what I want to know, Paul. Can I please speak to Mary?" Liam asked.

"Sure, Liam, please come in, but she already said she doesn't know where Kate went."

Janet Garvey sat at the kitchen table, wearing her customary sad face, looking as gloomy as the weeping clowns on the wallpaper in Kate's room.

"Liam needs to talk to Mary; Kate has not come home yet," said Paul.

"I spoke with her," said Janet as she lit a smoke. "She said she does not know anything but you go on and talk to her, Liam. I'm sure Kate is off somewhere in the neighborhood. I bet she's at the Doll Hospital." Liam politely listened, knowing that Kate did not play with dolls.

Mary was sitting cross-legged on her bed amid her record collection. Her father stood in the door, watching, as Liam pulled up the chair from Mary's desk and sat in front of her, with Bobby Darin a silent observer watching from the closet door.

"Mary, how long have I known you?" asked Liam.

"My whole life Mr. Dunn," said Mary, inserting Paul Anka back into a record sleeve.

"I need to know where Kate went," said Liam, absent the cop voice.

"All I know is she said she was going shopping and that she would see me at Mass tonight."

"Now for the tricky question. Do you know why I am not going out of mind right now, Mary?" asked Liam through a half smile.

Mary looked up coyly at Liam. "I was wondering about that, Mr. Dunn." Paul Garvey wondered to, but he kept the thought to himself.

"Because you are not going out of your mind, Mary, that's why. And that is because you know that your friend Kate is safe, and you know where she went."

"Mary," said her father, "I know Kate is your best friend, but you need to tell us where she is."

"I saw her coming out of Brian Kelly's law office," said Mary's brother Andy, standing behind their dad. Liam spun around. Andy sheepishly walked in the room with Colleen.

"Please, tell Liam what you told me, Andy," said Colleen urgently.

"She," Andy looked at his sister. "Gee Mr. Dunn, I feel like a rat."

"She got sick," said Colleen rescuing Andy.

"What do you mean ... sick?" asked Liam more than suspiciously.

"She threw up in the alley next to Tip Top Printing," said Colleen, fully aware of what was playing out on their last Christmas Eve in Washington Heights. Her husband's contrived plan not to discuss the move to Hicksville with his children and family until after Christmas was melting away as quickly as a spring snow.

"I hope she feels better, Liam," said Paul.

"Thanks Andy," said Liam, sliding the chair back in place, "and thanks Paul. Sorry to be a nuisance."

22

Kate gritted her teeth and looked up at the clock housed atop the water tower in Highbridge Park, a disgruntled resident with pigeons for neighbors. It ceased functioning three years ago and deceptively read a quarter past twelve. The clock's chimes, an honest set of bells, pealed six times in a shrill voice. She took pleasure in knowing her father would be irate and his anger compounded because she had not made the mandatory check-in phone call that he insisted on.

Kate began to run on the twisted path that snaked through the small urban forest, with her boots pounding out a steady cadence. She stopped beneath the stone archway at the entrance to the park and then slowly walked on to Amsterdam Avenue. She kicked over abandoned snow forts and knocked the head off a snowman standing guard at the bus stop before she sprinted the last three blocks to Wadsworth Avenue, where the wind waited to deliver a slap across her face.

The super of 86 Wadsworth had shoveled his stoop and seasoned it with the rock salt that crunched under Kate's feet. Saturating steam heat soaked the air turning the vestibule into a Turkish bath. She tore down the laughing plastic Santa attached to the door and scampered up the stairs where the deceased bulb in the stairwell leading to the roof generated a beckoning black hole. Entombed in darkness, Kate climbed the marble steps with her arms extended in front of her like a lost sleepwalker.

The buildings, 86 and 650, shared a common roof. The design likened them to Siamese twins, joined at the hip, creating an alley crisscrossed with clotheslines. She pushed against the snow-blocked door that stubbornly yielded an inch. The Freeze, always ready to create a nuisance, screeched through the ajar door and whistled like an angry teapot. Kate continued to assault the door until it finally gave way. She squeezed herself through the narrow opening and stumbled on to the roof. Without warning the chimney atop 650 erupted with a ferocious roar, discharging a cloud of black smoke that promised to suffocate her and erase her vision. Gasping, Kate struggled to her feet, rubbing her burning eyes, and searched for an escape route.

A gust of wind arrived that mercifully converted the smoke into a vortex that danced around her, cleansing the air. Kate's friends, the scarecrow antennas, appeared: caught in the gale, they pitched from port to starboard. Their umbilical cords of antenna wire cracked against the scaly brick skin of 650 like a teamster's whip. The eddy of smoke spun around the entrance to the roof before jettisoning off into the night sky, seemingly poking a hole in the clouds, allowing Kate to be bathed in moonlight. The sight of the stars activated her mental compass. She looked up and over her shoulder, due north. Polaris peeked from behind a cloud and ushered Orion's Belt to its reserved seat above the Loews Theatre.

Kate was the air traffic controller in apartment thirty-one. Nothing took off or landed without her detecting it. But not even the muffled conversations that slipped from behind the French doors of her parents' bedroom, which she so carefully monitored, lent a hint as to what was unfolding. Her dream of attending SHM had been suddenly destroyed like a sand castle struck by a wave. She had become ensnared in a web spun by others that left Kate for the first time in her young life, a life filled with accomplishments, struggling to comprehend what her future would bring.

Kate's attention turned toward the clotheslines strung around her like a bowl of Mrs. Carlo's spaghetti. She opened the toolbox Flann kept on the roof for antenna repairs and rummaged through it, pushing aside rusty screwdrivers, and left-over nuts and bolts. She picked up a pair of wire cutters and studied the rope lines. She decided she would keep the promise she had made on Danny's Straw Spider Day and create a web, a farewell web to Washington Heights.

She went to work cutting down the rope lines, ten feet from the first and eight feet from the second. Minutes later, Kate had over two hundred feet of rope. She quickly collected the rope and then dropped it over the edge of the roof and watched as it disappeared into the darkness.

■ ■ ■

Kate climbed down the ladder on the fire escape into the alley. She conducted a quick survey. The clothes lines Flann had strung between the windows on the ground floor would serve as the perfect anchor for her web.

Kate pushed through the hip-deep snow, weaving the rope around the existing lines until the snow in the alley looked like a freshly plowed field. The Freeze converted each breath she exhaled into a frozen fog that quickly vanished. She picked up the pace, creating the biggest web anyone could have imagined in Washington Heights.

Kate had kept the name of her Straw Spider secret for the past seven years, not even telling Mary when she gave up the name of her Straw Spider. She considered making a wish, but then laughed out loud to herself. That was a silly game that no longer existed. Her past now seemed so distant with the move to Hicksville, her surprise Christmas present that destroyed the future she had envisioned and meticulously planned. *Besides,* she thought, *the Straw Spiders could never grant the wish I would make.*

A loud thump startled Kate, followed by another and then another. The mysterious thumping continued until a ball of Grimes's cotton candy twine landed at her feet. Kate picked up the red ball. Its warmth penetrated her woolen gloves and the aroma from the cotton candy filled the air, and for an instant Kate's thoughts strolled through Palisades Amusement Park, realizing that too would be a place stripped from her life.

"I hope I didn't hit you," said Grimes as she climbed down the fire escape ladder, her words transporting Kate back into the alley. She watched as Grimes adjusted the belt on her tan raincoat. The black turban with the angel had replaced the green one, and half of her face remained hidden behind the heart-shaped carnival glasses.

"I see you have spun a Straw Spider web. Impressive Kate. I like the idea of the clothes line," said Grimes, inspecting the web.

"I said I was going to do it and I did. I finish what I say I'm going to do," replied Kate, letting the cotton candy ball drop from her hands.

"Yes, I heard you on Straw Spider Day whisper to yourself that it would be as strong as the power plant you built."

"Turns out to be a goodbye present to 650."

"A good-bye?" asked Grimes as she picked up three balls of twine and began to joggle them.

"Yes, my parents decided they wanted a house and bought one without even discussing it with their children, whose lives they are going to ruin," said Kate unamused by Grimes' circus act.

"People move all of the time Kate," replied Grimes, "I doubt very much all of their lives were ruined. I moved every three days and my life was certainly not ruined."

"I hardly think your life in a circus is anything like having to start my life over."

Grimes cradled the balls of twine in her arms and began to prowl around the alley like the cat who lived there in the summer. She caressed the rope web and gave it a gentle tug. "Your life will at times, feel very much like a circus, Kate. The acts will come and go. Some will excite the crowd, and others," said Grimes softly, "others won't be asked to move on to the next town."

"I have no choice in the matter. I must move to the next town. A town called Hicksville. How appropriate. Hicksville. Like Monica Broome asked me, 'Who wants to be a hick?'"

"And because of this move that you think is going to ruin your life, that's why you spun this web that is not a Straw Spider web but a farewell present?"

"That's right. I don't believe in Flann's ridiculous Straw Spiders ... I played along for my little brother's sake. We all did. My parents and my brother Rory. Just like the cookies on Christmas Eve and the magic key story I made up. The key that opens all doors. What a joke!"

"I liked that story. Danny was telling me about that. Very original, Kate. He also recited the poem you wrote about the fire in the chimney not being out. Very nice. Really, a fine effort. But I did hear you. I heard you whisper in the Cloisters that if it snowed, which I successfully predicted, you would create a web. And since you made this impressive web, I think you should honor it with a Straw Spider wish.

"Why? Why make a wish that could never come true? That would be a wasted wish if there ever was one," said Kate.

Grimes tied the end of the red ball of cotton candy twine to Kate's clothesline web. "Would you mind if I added my twine, Kate?"

"You can do whatever you want Miss Grimes. I'm finished with it and Christmas," said Kate as she walked out of the alley.

Grimes tossed her twine up and over Kate's rope lines in a magical game of catch, weaving the red and then the white and the blue into the web, inventing knots along the way. "But I already have, Kate. I have made a wish," replied Grimes to herself.

23

Liam sat in the dark and waited for Kate's call. He flipped the lid of his lighter open and shut and then spun the flint wheel with his thumb and watched as the blue flame appeared and licked the air around it casting shadows on the bedroom wall.

"Maybe you should just tell us what's going on Mom."

"Excellent idea, Rory," said Kate, her voice quivering.

Liam snapped the lid of his lighter shut at the sound of his daughter's voice.

Kate looked up at her father. The vomit-soiled scarf hung limply over her shoulders. Her hair, whisked into a frenzy by the wind no longer framed her face braised a ruddy red by The Freeze. "Don't ever do that again Kate. Ever. Do you understand me?" said Liam, able to breathe now that his daughter was home.

"You're worried about a phone call while my whole life has been turned upside down!" wailed Kate.

"Your life is about to get a whole lot better, Kate, and once you find yourself living in our own house, you will come to see that," lectured Liam.

"Do you really believe that? Do you have any idea what I will look like walking around the halls of Hicksville High School? A freak, that's what I'll look like! Everything will be different. I'm going to look like a clown."

"And what, Kate," said Liam, his anger building, "you were suddenly going to grow five inches at SHM?"

"Liam please," said Colleen. Hearing Liam use the height issue as a weapon stung.

"At SHM, I'd be wearing my uniform. I would look like everyone else! I would have fit in and I would be with Mary!" screamed Kate.

"You're going to make new friends," retorted Liam.

"I don't need new friends. I need to go to SHM, but you can't understand that. None of you can!"

Danny scampered into the kitchen with Dart in his hand, followed by Grandma and Grandpa. Rory had secured the Godzilla damaged wing with fresh tape. Liam snared him as he flew past the window and placed him on the washing machine, the temporary hangar for Danny and Dart.

"And when were you going to announce that we are moving to Hicksville?" asked Kate sarcastically.

"Moving? Who the hell is moving?" Grandpa dropped his sleigh bells on the floor and himself into a chair, not wanting to believe a word he was hearing.

"We are, Grandpa. The Dunn family is moving out," said Kate, no longer able to stop the flood of tears streaming down her face.

"Moving on," corrected Liam.

"Hauling ass out of here is what it sounds like to me," said Rory as he entered the kitchen.

Colleen picked up the sleigh bells, placed them in her father's lap, and assumed the role of cheerleader. "Hicksville High School is one of the best schools in the state of New York," she said. "Its brand-new Katherine with science and language labs and a big library, bigger than the one on 179th Street. And wait until you see the football field Rory, no more taking the subway to Van Cortland Park."

"I like the subway, and I like Van Cortland Park," said Rory.

Shannon clung to the Jon Gnagy pad and peeked into the kitchen from the hallway. *It was happening again,* thought Shannon. But this time the Dunn's were leaving her, like the TV and the toaster banished to the repair shop.

"They even have their own practice field and the home field has lights like Yankee Stadium! How about that, Rory?" boasted Liam.

"What makes you think I'll make the team if they are so great?" asked a dejected Rory.

"I'm going to have Brother Anthony speak to the coach of Hicksville. You are just as good as any of them, if not better."

"So, what you're telling me is the next game I play will be my last game with All Hallows?"

"That's exactly what he's saying Rory, and I'm not going to SHM am I Dad?" asked Kate wiping her tear streaked cheeks with the scarf.

"No, Kate you aren't. We will be moving in June, and you and Rory will be going to Hicksville High School. I know it's not what you want to hear, but it will be for the best, and the sooner you come to terms with that, the better off you will be," said Liam.

"How about that, Katherine?" said Colleen. "Having your big brother in the same school with you for two years? And Danny, you will be taking the school bus to your school right next to the high school."

"I want to go to Incarnation. Next year, I will have Sister Elaine, and I like her."

Grandpa buried his face in his hands and moaned, "You're putting my granddaughter in with dem' heathen Prods?"

"And EYE-TALIANS," said Kate aping her grandfather, "Lots of them are moving to Hicksville, classes full of them!"

"Denying her of a Catholic education Liam – God almighty talk some sense into your daughter Bridget!" pleaded Grandpa.

"This family will be land owners again," said Grandma pushing her eyeglasses back up the bridge of her nose. "A fine job, Colleen and congratulations to ya Liam. Proud of ya both, I am."

"Grandma, please! Don't you understand we are moving to Hicksville? Away from you and Grandpa!?" said Kate, fully exasperated.

"I'm understandin' that my daughter and my beloved granddaughter will be peelin' potatoes in their own kitchen, and my son-in-law will be payin' down the mortgage and not loadin' the pockets of the landlord. 'Tis a good thing, for sure, to be ownin' a home."

"Hicksville Grandma. I bet you have no idea where that is," said a fuming Kate.

"It's on Long Island Grandma," said Shannon, trying to be helpful.

"Please Shannon she doesn't need any help!" yelled Kate.

"'Tirty' five minutes from the Pennsylvania train station and not a minute more," answered Grandma proudly.

"How would ya know that?" asked Grandpa.

"Maureen O'Brien, from the old neighborhood. Ya must be re-memberin' the O'Brien's and their daughter Femora, who broke her father's heart when she married the Pollack fireman. Sat next to Maureen I did, at the Dunleavy wake. And would ya be knowin' they go once a month to visit their daughter and ya should know Mr. O'Brien is gettin' on grand with the Pollack son in law. Growin' tomatoes together, they are. 'Tis a fine thing for sure. And Hicksville be where they bought the house."

The Dunn's became a cast of muted actors. The ticking cat clock played the overture, while they waited for a cue from the wings to prompt the stalled scene. Each time Grandpa glanced in Colleen's direction, his daughter found an excuse to perform a meaningless task, touching this thing or that thing, moving the Christmas towel draped over the sink an unnecessary inch to the right.

"I know there is something you want more than anything else in the world Danny," said Colleen, breaking the Benedictine silence that shrouded them.

Here it comes thought Kate. *The bribe.* It was so obvious to her now. She could hear Lassie yelping.

"You do?" asked Danny.

"What if I told you we were adding a new member to the family?" teased Colleen.

"What? Aunt Colleen is going to have a baby?" asked a confused Shannon.

"Good lord, Shannon! Keep those thoughts to yourself," said a gasping Grandpa.

"Well," Colleen hopped up on the washing machine next to Danny, "a puppy is like a baby, and Danny will be like a big brother too, so let me guess: what will you name him, Danny. Lassie?"

"We're getting a dog!" exclaimed Danny dropping Dart.

Liam snuffed out his cigarette, "Yep and Mom's getting her driver's license, and next year, Rory can get his learner's permit."

"I can?" Rory's voice suddenly regained its strength.

"Sure, you can," said an upbeat Liam. "And seniors can drive to school."

"Well, that is kind of cool," said Rory, avoiding the scorching stare from his sister.

"When? When are we going to get Lassie?" asked an elated Danny.

"The day after we move in, we will go to the kennel and get a dog," said Liam.

"I can't wait. And we need a leash and a bowl, right Dad?" asked Danny.

"Sure, do Danny," said Liam.

"Backyard be fine for a dog," opined Grandma.

"We're on an eighty-by-a- hundred lot. Big back yard! Three bedrooms and I am going to add two more rooms upstairs. They designed the house for expansion. We can do the work ourselves, me and Rory, and you too Grandpa. We can frame it out and sheet rock it," exclaimed an excited Liam.

Kate looked at her day dreaming big brother. *Judas*, thought Kate, the thirty pieces of silver replaced by a used car. "I could keep my football equipment in the trunk," said Rory.

"And the cock crowed three times, Rory," said Kate stomping out of the room.

The doorbell rang. Danny slid off the washing machine and dashed out of the kitchen. "Hi, Aunt Nora." The sound of Danny's voice drew Shannon like iron ore to a magnet. A pleasant sight greeted her and it amazed her. Her mom's hair was pulled neatly back and mimicked Colleen's. The little make-up she wore freshened her face, replacing her dreary look.

"Merry Christmas," said Nora, following Danny and Shannon into the kitchen, even though there was little merriment in her life. Nora put down two shopping bags, one filled with stocking stuffers wrapped in white paper napkins secured with rubber bands. A large box, beautifully wrapped in glossy silver paper and a fancy twenty-cent red bow, caught Shannon's attention. It had a gift tag that read, "To Shannon from Dad."

Shannon had worried about who would be showing up with her mother. Ernie or Dad? With the question answered, that neither one would be spending Christmas with her, she retreated to Kate's room.

"Your brother is moving his family to Bicksville," said Grandpa.

"Hicksville Dad," Colleen corrected him.

"Bicksville, Hicksville who cares? All I know is you're breaking up the family."

"You're moving, Liam?" asked Nora as she began fumbling around in her pocket book.

"Yes Nora, we are moving. My wife and I have committed the mortal sin of buying a house and now his Holiness Father Grandpa Finn is very upset."

"Well I'm happy for you both," said Nora, freshening her lipstick. "It turns out that I don't have to leave the apartment so I will be staying in Brooklyn for the time being."

"I'm going to teach my dog all kinds of tricks. He'll be the smartest Lassie ever," said Danny.

"Mom, is it alright if I wrap Kate's present in your room?"

"Sure," said Colleen, "and then you can be first up in the bathroom. We will be on our way to Mass at eleven-thirty," said Colleen.

"Eleven-fifteen if we want to sit in a pew," said Grandpa barely above a whisper.

24

Danny buckled the strap on the Johnnie Blast flying helmet under his chin and pulled the goggles over his eyes. He knew it would be cold in Dart's cockpit, so he wrapped Rory's scarf around his neck. He pushed Dart past the fire truck Santa had brought last Christmas and turned into a toy gas station, where he fueled Dart and his fleet of cars.

"Have to fill up Dart," said Danny, holding the miniature nozzle on to his plane. He taxied the glider on the wooden floor runway and came to a stop. He required clearance to take off, just as Sky King did.

"This is Dart, ready for takeoff," said Danny to the platoon of toy soldiers standing in formation on Rory's bed.

"Roger, Captain Dunn, clear to take off," replied Danny loudly to himself in his deepest voice.

He slid his toy chest across the room, as happy a baggage handler as there ever was. He climbed aboard the chest, grabbed his hockey stick, placed it under the window's wood frame, and slowly pushed it up. The Freeze slithered into the room, coiling itself around him like a boa constrictor. He leaned out the window and into the darkness, the way he had watched his mother do so many times. He fastened the glider to the rope line with a clothespin and launched Dart across the alley. Danny's passengers arrived at the terminal at the other end of the rope. After a short stay, he ordered them back on board and began to retrieve Dart. The glider emerged from the darkness, barely illuminated by the light emanating from his room. The pulley seized up, forcing Dart into a holding pattern above the alley.

Frustrated, Danny clambered on to the windowsill. He steadied himself and stretched his tiny torso over the window guard meant to protect him. He smiled when his finger touched the balsa wood plane. A cracking sound startled him when the screws tore free from their mooring. Danny Dunn, a wingless cherub, plummeted into the abyss.

■ ■ ■

Liam was right, mused Colleen. They were good. As good, as they could be, after the news of the move to Hicksville broke prematurely. She placated herself with pleasant scenarios as she removed her special Christmas-themed dish from the cupboard, which her Danny would soon be stacking with cookies for Saint Nicholas.

She considered her mother's encouraging words to be a wonderful Christmas present. Rory's restrained excitement about driving was certainly a good omen of things to come, along with Danny being so enthralled, as she had expected, with thoughts of his very own Lassie. She remained concerned about her daughter and prayed that once Katherine entered Hicksville High School and learned all it had to offer, she would take her place as one of the best students and make lots of new friends. Colleen smiled as she wiped the dish, her thoughts retuning to Lassie playing with Danny in the Dunn back yard.

The Freeze hugged the hallway floor and crawled into the kitchen. A sudden chill latched on to Colleen, distracting her from the ongoing chatter in the room. Nora, jabbering about the job she hoped one day to have. Grandpa, lamenting about the move to "Bicksville." Colleen mentally exhaled her concern with The Freeze lapping at her feet. Katherine must be talking out of the window with Mary. "Liam," said Colleen softly, "would you please ask Katherine to use the phone and not the window?"

"I'll be takin' care of it," said Grandma happily, still overjoyed about her daughter's new home. She returned before Colleen had the Santa cookie dish on the table. "Ya will find your daughter under her bed, and Shannon 'tis working at the easel. Lord, that child can paint."

"Did you close the window?" Colleen asked.

"Kate's window was closed," said Grandma.

The excruciating scream continued until Colleen's lungs collapsed. The agonizing aria pierced the souls of the tenants, only ending after a deathlike stillness draped itself over 650. Happy Christmas conversations stopped mid-sentence, and the radios fell silent. The Yule log burned on TV screens absent the voices of a choir. The tenants waited, haunted by what they had heard. Then the scream returned, louder, uglier, dragging with it a name... Danny.

25

The hospital's Presbyterian chapel was a desert compared to those of Kate's Roman Catholic roots. There were no candles to light in front of Jesus or his Blessed Mother or the stained-glass windows that celebrated the lives of the saints. The oasis, shared by both faiths, was the cross on the chapel's wooden altar. Kate prepared herself for prayer the way the nuns had taught her to pray, as Jesus did when confronted by his enemy, Satan. She would not temp the creator of the universe to perform a miracle, easily sparing Danny's life. Kate prayed instead for the strength to accept the will of the Lord and whatever that brought.

The day's sickening events played on in her mind in the same sequential order, and trapped Kate on a carousel of despair. Once more, she watched herself running down the stairs behind her mother and father and then obeying Liam's order to stay back when they got close to Danny. The vision of Danny lying in the snow next to the Straw Spider web caused the gut-wrenching sobs to return. Once again, she found herself riding in the patrol car between Rory and Shannon, racing behind the ambulance, with their sirens blaring.

Kate ran her hands through her hair and wiped the tears off her cheeks. Her effort to slow her breaths, which arrived in short gasps, failed. Rory entered the chapel. He sat next to Kate and, without speaking he knelt and buried his face in his hands.

"I never should have fixed that plane," said Rory, barely able to push out the words through his tears. "It never would have happened if I had just left that plane alone."

"Don't think that way, Rory," said Kate choking on her words.

"And you always worried that this would happen and now it did," said Rory fighting to regain his composure.

Kate hated the plane and hated herself for not stepping on it all those times Danny left it on the floor in her room. That would have closed Rory's repair shop. But none of that mattered. "We have to pray now, together Rory, for Danny," whispered Kate.

■ ■ ■

Nora sat at the kitchen table. The cat clock's paws read 12:10 a.m. Christmas was ten minutes old, and she had no idea what lay in store for the Dunn family. Not for the day or the week or the year. When the expected knock on the door arrived, she stood and put a set of rosary beads in her pocket.

Powers and Rodriguez followed Holden, the detective assigned to investigate Danny's fall, into apartment thirty-one. A photographer, the only unarmed man, walked with a pronounced limp and trailed behind them, lugging his equipment in a tattered brown suitcase.

Nora led them to Danny's room. Holden removed his black fedora and stood at rigid attention. The sentences shot from his mouth in annoying short spurts. "Sorry to hear about your nephew. I spoke with your brother. Everyone's upset. Whole department's upset. Everyone is praying. For the boy."

"Thank you," replied Nora.

Holden cast a wary eye over the bedroom and removed a tape measure from his pocket as the photographer loaded a flashbulb into his camera.

Years on the job had taught him not to assume anything, even if the father of the boy involved in the incident was a cop. He glanced at the toy
chest that remained by the clothespin bag under the window. The hockey
stick stood propped against the wall, the way Danny had left it. Unlike his
speech pattern, his movement within the room was methodically slow.
Holden measured the distance from the bed to the chest and from the top
of the chest to the windowsill.

He lifted the lid of the toy chest reverently, as if he were opening a cas-
ket. The jack-in-the-box delivered a near-knockout blow. His son played
with an identical toy. It took all of Holden's strength to remain a cop in
front of cops and conceal his emotions. A life parallel to that of Holden's
six-year-old emerged. The slinky, toy soldiers and Mr. Machine. He softly
touched a cigar box filled with Danny's cherished marbles. After a silent, ten- second pause, he stepped back. The lame photographer hobbled
around the chest, took three pictures, and then stood, lopsided, and waited
for Holden's instructions.

"Get a shot of the hockey stick," said Holden in rapid fire, afraid his
voice might crack.

Nora stepped away from the room, leaned against the hallway wall,
and studied the floor.

"Your nephew used this hockey stick to open the window?" asked
Holden holding the stick, back in control.

"That's what we think," said Nora barely above a whisper, as if she
were in a confessional booth.

Holden went back to work with his tape measure and jotted down his
calculations on a small pad. The photographer began taking photos of
the room from every conceivable angle and created a lightning storm of
exploding flash bulbs.

Nora looked into the room; she fought with the image of Danny tum-
bling into the alley. She turned away when Holden opened the window,
letting The Freeze flood the room. He stroked the wood frame and then
barked out his next order.

"Get the screw holes."

The photographer focused on the jagged gaping holes in the wood frame. Content with his dozen shots he limped to his suitcase. Holden carefully examined the pulley. He attempted to move the clothesline, but it remained stuck. He pulled harder on the line, but it refused to cooperate.

Holden had questions for Flann, who led the cops and the limping photographer into the alley.

"What's this?" asked Holden as he pointed his flashlight at Kate's Straw Spider web spun with rope and Grimes's twine.

Flann studied the cop as he lit his pipe. "Oh, 'tis just one of those silly webs the kids weave at Christmas time. Ya know, makin' a wish sort a thing."

Holden tugged on the web. "Just curious. Who made this one?" he asked.

Obviously, Grimes had a hand in weaving the web, 'tis her cotton candy twine all over the alley, thought Flann. And Kate Dunn, Flann would have bet his life that it was her handy work. There was nothing about the web that appeared childlike or haphazard. She might as well have put her signature on the web. But he would not be giving up his passengers to the cops. "No idea; could have been any of a dozen kids," said Flann, puffing on his pipe. Holden began to walk a cop's beat around the web, looking for anything that might present itself as being suspicious. His attention turned to a small ball of Grimes's red twine. He picked it up, uncoiled a length of the twine, and wrapped it around his hands and performed a quick tensile test, giving it a solid tug.

The photographer popped a picture of the orange outline the ambulance crew had spray painted around little Danny before they'd placed him on the stretcher. Holden paused and then slowly measured the distance from the web to where Danny had landed. Holden looked above his head and discovered a broken clothesline that emerged from a second-floor window and dangled four feet above the concrete. He reasoned to himself that Danny hit the line, which broke his fall, and that was why the boy, for the moment, was still alive. He'd investigated over a dozen window accidents. There had been no survivors from the height Danny had fallen from; not one, ever.

"Okay. Few shots of the alley. Then we will be on our way. Let Liam know. We are thinking of him. And his family," blurted Holden.

Rodriguez took out a smoke, and Powers did the same. Powers lit both their cigarettes, then turned up the collar on his jacket, never taking his eyes off Rodriguez who was slowly walking around the alley. Powers took a hit on his smoke as Rodriguez paced off the distance from the wall to the web. The two cops quickly understood what Holden must have noted on his pad.

26

Liam and Colleen stood in front of the chief of neurology Doctor Hanks, who delivered information in a slow and measured way, like an intravenous drip. "There is some swelling, a fluid buildup. Medically speaking, it is normal for this condition to present itself under these circumstances. I see no reason to drain the fluid, but we will monitor it closely, and if we need to intervene, to remove any pressure, we will do so."

"I want to see my Danny," said Colleen.

"Yes, of course," said Hanks, turning toward Liam. "I have placed Danny in a medically induced coma. We are going to rest his brain, calm things down."

"How long will he stay in this, induced coma?" said Liam barely audibly.

"For at least the next forty-eight hours. We will be able to see if the fluid around the brain is decreasing. Amazingly, all we are certain of is a broken left arm."

"I want to see him. I need to see Danny now," repeated Colleen.

"Yes, of course. He is comfortable; he is unaware of the tubes and equipment. So please, understand that he is not in any pain."

"Thank you, doctor," said Liam.

Colleen fainted when she entered the room.

Grandpa sat in the waiting area of the hospital. When he tried to speak, he wept, and so he stopped speaking. Grandma had gone upstairs to see Danny. Kate, Rory, and Shannon could not go upstairs, because the sign on the wall said visitors had to be sixteen and the old man working at the receptionist desk enforced the rule. And so they each sat on a pink plastic chair, inhaling the antiseptic smell that permeated the air, and silently prayed for Danny, knowing Grandma would be back in twenty minutes. She came back every twenty minutes, and every twenty minutes she reported, "Danny is still asleep."

The cops gathered in the lobby wanted to give blood. A nurse told them that Danny did not need blood, but that the hospital always needed blood. So, many of the cops followed her into a room and they gave their blood. A cop from the Three-Four on Wadsworth Avenue told Rory that when midnight Mass ended at Incarnation no one left. Everyone, he said, stayed, and prayed for Danny Dunn. He reported that people were coming and going all day long and that the church was practically full.

He looked at Grandpa and said that the monsignor told him that all the Christmas Masses would be for Danny. That is what the cop told Grandpa, who could not reply.

■ ■ ■

Reporters monitoring police frequencies picked up the news of Danny's fall and alerted the AP wire service. The three network news channels, every radio station, and all the major newspapers covered the story. It was front-page news in the New York City papers sold at Pedro's newsstand that the feisty Puerto Rican's brother was looking after. Pedro was at Incarnation Church, sitting next to Jimmy the Jerk and told his wife they would not be leaving the church until Danny woke up.

Everyone in the country knew of the plight of little Danny Dunn, including Colleen's brother, Connor Dolan, stepping out of a taxi in front of the hospital with his wife Maria. As soon as they entered the lobby, he spotted his father. Maria squeezed his hand, a reminder of the promise that he had made to her, there would not be any arguments. Maria had made it clear that all that mattered was the little nephew they had never met and Conor's sister and mother, whom Connor sorely missed.

He instantly recognized the boy standing in the corner of the lobby. The last time he'd seen Rory he had been eight. He had grown into the image of Conor's brother-in-law: the hair, the chin, the nose. When Rory began to walk over, Connor saw that he carried himself like Liam, his shoulders back and his head up, simulating the young Marine he remembered his sister dating.

He watched as his nephew took a seat next to a girl. "Look," whispered Connor, "that must be Katherine."

"She looks like Colleen," replied Maria.

Kate watched the man approaching her. He looked familiar, and then she recognized her uncle from the picture he enclosed in the Christmas card he sent each year. This year, the photograph of the Dolan's was at Disneyland, in front of the Dumbo ride, which made the Dunn children jealous and confirmed that her two cousins had truly escaped the short curse she had inherited from their grandparents. Connor, like during everyone's first encounter with Kate, found himself trapped in a pool of quicksand, mesmerized by her penetrating blue eyes.

"You must be Katherine," said Connor. Kate could sense his awkwardness and quickly stood up.

"Yes, and you're our Uncle Connor. I recognize you from the picture. And Aunt Maria."

"Hello Katherine," said Maria extending her hand.

"You can call me Kate, everyone does, except my mom." *So*, thought Kate. *This is the Eye-Talian my uncle married in defiance of his father's wishes.* She was even more beautiful in person then she was in the picture, in which Kate thought she looked like a movie star.

"Hello Dad."

The old man looked up at the couple who were strangers to Kate, Rory and Shannon. Finn struggled to his feet. "I wouldn't blame you if you didn't shake my hand," he said.

Maria stepped forward and took Grandpa in her arms, "Let this end," she whispered in his ear.

"How could you ever forgive me for my stupid behavior?" asked Finn, afraid to return her embrace.

"It's over... I want it to be over and so does your son and our children," said Maria stepping back.

Finn put out his hand, which Connor pushed aside as he embraced his father. His mother entered the lobby accompanied by two cops and a priest. Her overcoat with the mismatched buttons flooded his mind with memories as she walked toward him.

"Connor!" said Grandma almost losing her balance.

"We came as soon as we heard about Danny on the news." Maria spoke in a hushed voice the way people do in hospitals.

Maria stepped into Grandma's open arms. "Thank God you are here with Connor," whispered Grandma.

"How is Colleen doing, and Liam?" asked Maria, wiping her tears away with the back of her hand.

"Doing as best they can for sure. Grandma turned to the priest. "Father Doyle let me introduce ya to our son Connor and his wife Maria." It was the closest Connor had been to a priest in ten years and now he regretted that too. "Father," said Conner, shaking the old priest's hand.

"Sorry we have to meet under these circumstances," said the priest, who turned toward the elevator that announced its arrival with a gentle chime. "Let me be on my way."

"Yes, thank ya Father, and we will be right along," said Grandma.

"I cannot believe what 'tis happening, I'm just..."

The Dolan children had never seen their mother cry. Her secret crying place was in the bathroom, where she had camouflaged her sobs by opening the bathtub faucets when the letters had arrived from Ireland bringing the news of the death of a brother and then a sister. She had reappeared, composed, when the water finally shut off, and then the Dolan's were off to church to light candles and say the proper prayers.

Grandma led the way out of the elevator passing white-uniformed nurses, who stepped aside and gave a polite nod to the family of Danny Dunn. She stopped at the door of the hospital room and turned to Connor and Marie.

"Ya need to know that your sister has not spoken a word since Danny..." Grandma struggled to complete the sentence.

"It's okay, Mom, we understand," said Maria.

Connor stepped into the hospital room. The low beeping sound of the machine attached to Danny arrived with each breath. Danny's face looked tranquil and no different from when he slipped off to sleep on Liam's lap after a bedtime story. Father Doyle was not quite sure and kept the thought to himself, but it appeared as if Danny had the slightest smile on his pink lips.

Colleen was resting her head on the bed, her hair partially hiding the wooden splint on Danny's arm. Connor placed his hand on Colleen's shoulder. She looked up at her brother, and her tears rolled down her cheeks. Connor kissed her forehead. Colleen said nothing and placed her head back on the bed.

■ ■ ■

The nuns of Incarnation, led by Sister Mary of the Crucifix arrived at 7:00 p.m. The man at the reception desk said the twelve nuns needed permission to be in the room with Danny. Sister Mary of the Crucifix asked the man politely to get the required permission. When he left, the nuns went up the stairwell to the third floor where Father Doyle told them Danny's room was located.

"Mrs. Dunn," said Sister Mary softly, poking her head in the door, "the sisters have come to see Danny, if that would be all right."

Colleen continued her silence, so Grandma stood up. "That would be fine Sister."

The nuns filed into the room and circled Danny's bed. Danny's favorite sister, Sister Elaine, led the rosary. The nurses working on the third floor stopped what they were doing and stood outside the door and prayed with the nuns for Danny.

After the rosary, Sister Pauline gave Grandma a big basket with special prayer offering cards the members of Incarnation Church had purchased. There were over four hundred cards.

27

THE SECOND DAY OF CHRISTMAS, DECEMBER 27. THE VIGIL.

Danny did not wake up. Doctor Hanks never assured them that he would awaken when he ended the induced coma, but Danny's family thought that would happen, and when it didn't, they became distraught. Doctor Hanks reported that there was brain activity and that Danny's vital signs were strong, and said he would be removing the respirator later in the day.

A nurse brought a washbasin and told Colleen she could wash Danny's face. Colleen wished the water in the basin were a tad warmer. Liam watched as she gently dabbed the washcloth on Danny's forehead. He was not certain at first, but he thought Danny's pinkie, on his right hand moved ever so slightly. Grandpa could not have seen it. His head had dropped down to his chest, indicating he would be fitfully asleep for five minutes. The priest sat in the corner, reading his missal. Grandma had gone to show Connor, Marie, and Nora where the waiting room was that allowed smoking.

Liam moved to the right side of Danny's bed. He knelt and studied the little finger. Colleen thought he was praying. Then there was no doubt the finger moved, maybe an eighth of an inch.

"Colleen," he said. She continued administering the tepid water to Danny's face. "Colleen, look at me."

Colleen turned toward Liam as she dipped the washcloth back in the water. He wished he could tell her they were good, but he couldn't; not yet anyway.

"Danny's pinkie moved," said Liam.

Father Doyle stopped reading. Grandpa woke with a startled look on his face. Grandma entered the room and immediately sensed something was astir.

"And what might be goin' on?" asked Grandma.

Colleen spoke her first words in two days. "Liam said Danny's pinkie moved."

"Finn … go quick and tell the nurses," said Grandma urgently.

A flurry of activity erupted at the third-floor nurses station. Liam could hear the page that broadcasted throughout the hospital on the public-address system. "Doctor Hanks. Doctor Hanks. Third floor, Doctor Hanks."

"Talk to him Mrs. Dunn. Talk to him," said the nurse.

"Danny… Danny its Mom. Please, Danny, open your eyes. I know you can. Please come back."

Doctor Hanks entered the room with the three resident doctors he was conducting rounds with.

"Mr. Dunn thinks he saw Danny's pinkie move," reported the nurse.

"It did. Barely, but it did," said Liam enthusiastically.

Doctor Hanks removed a medical flashlight from his pocket and lifted Danny's eyelid.

"Refraction perfectly normal," said the doctor.

Everyone saw it, as if a comet had streaked across a summer sky. This time two fingers moved. No one had to tell Colleen her job.

"Danny! Danny, its Mom! Please, Danny, open your eyes!"

The doctors removed Danny from the respirator, which stopped the beeping and laid a solemn silence over the room. Doctor Hanks was ready to begin the lecture he gave to the families of comatose patients, explaining that sometimes there are signs of improvement, like fingers or toes performing an involuntary motion. But then Danny became the show-stopper and opened his eyes.

"Danny!" cried Colleen. "Danny, can you hear me? Please tell me you can hear me!"

"I can hear you Mom,. His words were barely audible. "And I heard you calling me. You were calling me, weren't you?"

"Oh, yes. Yes, I was Danny. I was calling you and you heard me!"

"Can I please have a glass of water?" asked Danny in a faint raspy voice.

The nurse immediately placed a cup of ice water with a straw in front of Danny's lips. He took a long sip.

"Hi, Dad," said Danny, his voice stronger after the water. Liam knelt over Danny's broken arm and began to weep in waves of throbbing sobs. Doctor Hanks and his team of young physicians walked out of the room, knowing the Dunns were in the tender care of the nurses and a priest.

The news concerning Danny Dunn spread throughout the hospital and spilled out to the parking lot, where a police car stood its watch. The cop behind the wheel put out an all-point-bulletin that Danny Dunn was awake and well. The patrol cars in Washington Heights picked up the report and echoed the news. Within thirty minutes, the entire neighborhood knew Danny Dunn miraculously had survived the fall from a third-floor window.

Kate, Rory, and Shannon stepped off the elevator. Doctor Hanks relaxed the rules barring them from visiting Danny. They followed behind a nurse who led them quickly to Danny's room. He was free of the tubes and intravenous lines. The only indication of the fall was the splint on his arm.

"Danny, look who's here," said Colleen jubilantly.

Kate raced to the bed and hopped up next to Danny. "Hi, Kate," said Danny as if he had just invaded her room in violation of the Eleventh Commandment.

"Hi Danny," laughed Kate before a flood of tears washed over her cheeks.

The nurses got Danny out of bed, and everyone watched in amazement, as if he were taking his first baby steps. A walk to the door and back to the bed and Danny was like an old salt treading on the deck of a schooner.

Danny said his throat was a little sore, so the nurses brought him a bowl of ice cream that Jan's Ice Cream Parlor on Fordham Road would have been proud to serve. It was almost as big as the famous Kitchen Sink, which took six kids to devour.

Detectives Powers and Rodriguez showed up as representatives of the NYPD. They brought a copy of the *Journal American* newspaper. Danny's survival made front-page news and introduced Detective Holden to the city of New York. His final report concluded that Danny had landed on a spider-web type net constructed from clothesline rope that in turn acted like a trampoline, which explained how Danny wound up next to the rope net. The report also stated that Danny had been wearing a leather flying hat that absorbed a portion of the impact. Holden made special note of the fact that Danny struck two clotheslines that spanned the alley and that that largely contributed to his survival. He made no mention of the Grimes's cotton candy twine because that would lead to questions he had no answers for.

"Hey Danny, how's my man doing?" asked Powers.

"I'm doing okay. I guess you heard I fell out of the window," said Danny seriously.

Everyone laughed, Powers the loudest. "Yeah, Danny, I heard about it!"

Colleen sat on the bed. She was not yet ready to let go of Danny's hand.

"I'd like to know who built that net in alley?" asked Rodriguez.

Flann heard the question as he entered the room and was quick to offer an explanation. "That's not bein' a net 'tis a Straw Spider web, and I have to be tellin' ya the whole of Washington Heights be paradin' in and out of the alley to get a look at it."

"Hi, Flann," said Danny happily.

"And hello to ya Danny and I have to be tellin' ya that seein' ya lookin' so well is the finest Christmas present anyone could be gettin'."

"So tell us, Kate, any idea as to who might have created the web in the alley?" asked Liam.

"From the rope borrowed from the roof, no less," added Flann.

"The Straw Spiders of course. No doubt in my mind whatsoever. And like you always said Flann. 'Only speak of them and not about them' " replied Kate knowingly.

Colleen had Liam nail the window shut in her son's bedroom. It never opened again, and so the Linen Angel never returned to apartment thirty-one. She placed her sheets over two chairs in the kitchen and did so until the day the Dunns moved to Hicksville. How Danny survived the fall became a subject of debate throughout Washington Heights. Some believed it was the Johnnie Blast flying helmet. Liam doubted that, because it really was not a helmet, just a leather contraption that covered his head and ears.

Mike Hickey said most of his customers in the High Spot, who had expert opinions on everything, thought it was Danny hitting the rope clotheslines, and the two feet of snow in the alley that created a pillow. Flann had no doubt in his mind. It was the Straw Spider web and he forgave the web spinner for cutting down his clotheslines on the roof to make it, along with the cotton candy twine supplied by H. Wellington Grimes.

28

THE STRANGER

Big Jim Riley paused to light his smoke. His thoughts drifted to the news he'd heard about the Dunn kid surviving the fall, and he wished his grandson, who had died of cancer the year before, could have been as lucky. He continued his way up the cobble stone path that led to the Cloisters. He was ahead of his starting time; he made a habit of being just that for his midnight shift. It alleviated his concern about the subway being on time. And relieving the man working the middle shift a few minutes early was the way the men of the trench conducted their business.

The street lamp at the end of the path cast its light upon the figure of a man. It was not right at this hour, for anyone to be lingering about, and so Riley changed his course and slowly strode to another, more secluded entrance to the Cloisters.

The Stranger walked as fast as his aged legs could carry him, and he managed to come close to Riley, who thought he heard footsteps behind him. He turned to face the man.

"Jim Riley, I'm told that's ya name," said the man.

" 'Tis if that be any of your business," replied Big Jim sternly.

" 'Tis because I've seen with my own eyes that you are a friend to Flann McFarland of Belfast."

"I am for sure his friend and myself from Belfast," Big Jim was finding himself a bit intrigued.

"Then we're findin' ourselves with a thing in common, both with an interest in Flann McFarland. Both being from Belfast," said the Stranger.

Big Jim sensed he had nothing to fear from the man with the familiar brogue. Besides their being countrymen, he was bigger than the man in every way.

"Ya knew him back home, did ya?" asked the man as he took a step closer to Big Jim.

"I did, and his mother as well," said Big Jim, wondering what in God's name all the fuss over Flann might be.

"Did ya now... and what of his brother?"

"His brother died at the age of an hour."

"Ya sure of that are ya?"

"Flann's bein' a seanchai, the finest of story-tellers, but never a liar," said Big Jim.

"A man cannot lie about things he has no knowledge of," offered the man.

The Stranger stepped in front of Big Jim and removed his knitted cap. Big Jim looked closely at his face.

"Let's step into the light, Jim Riley so you can be seein' why I'm in need of yer help."

The Stranger followed Riley to the solid wood door that trapped every watt of light behind it. When the door cracked open, the light escaped and fell on the face of Tomas McFarland himself, alive and well, in Washington Heights.

■ ■ ■

Flann's two-room cave, cluttered with furniture and artwork left behind by tenants who had moved or died, sat next to the boiler room. The picture he had taken with Dwiggy on their wedding day rested on a table, next to the chair Timmy Gilmartin's sister gave him after her brother died.

Kate and Mary were tapping out messages on the steam pipes. The clinging and clanging had not stopped for the better part of an hour and was getting on Flann's nerves when the solid rap on his door arrived.

"And look who it might be, Jim Riley himself. Come on in, won't ya," said Flann.

"Yer lookin' fit for a man with one foot in the grave," joked Big Jim.

"Come on in now, easy enough to be findin' a seat here that's for sure," quipped Flann.

Big Jim plopped down in the chair left behind by the Pratt family when they moved to New Jersey. He silently said hello to The picture of Dwiggy that brought back memories of the day he stood as best man.

"So, what might be bringin' ya here? I hope I'm not owin' ya money, or worse, that your bride threw ya out and you're needin' a place to live. A little crowded it would be," said Flann.

"The truth 'tis… "

"Good to at least start with the truth," interrupted Flann while lighting his pipe.

"I'm bringin' ya news, Flann."

Flann McFarland had no fear of news, for he had not a soul in his life. He had the one brother, whom he never knew, and his Dwiggy, and both of them were long dead.

"Good news, I'm hopin' I won the sweepstakes," replied Flann.

"I met someone from home, Flann."

"Did ya now. And might I be knowin' em?"

"I have to be sayin' a yes and a no to that, Flann."

Flann puffed on his pipe; he enjoyed a riddle. "And a riddle 'tis it?"

"I've met someone, and I've brought him with me. He's right outside the door Flann."

" 'Tis he now?

Big Jim rose from the chair and opened the door. Tomas McFarland, Flann's identical twin, stepped into the room. Flann dropped his pipe. The bowl of the pipe cracked in half when it struck the cold concrete floor, spewing glowing embers.

"Flann," said Tomas. His voice, like his face was identical to Flann's. "I've come a long way to be findin' my brother."

"But I was told that ya had died."

"I might as well have been dead. Our ma and pa, it was no fault of theirs, forced, they were, to give one of us up. Twas the Hunger and ya know that story well."

"I do... but where did ya go?"

"The nuns took me in the day after we were born, and at the age of two, I was sent off to the south and adopted by what they thought were a fine family. I eventually got away. By that time, you had already left for America. I only found out about ya a few years back.

The oldest nun in the convent in Belfast told the story on her deathbed. A young novice heard of it, checked, and found a record of our births."

"And all these years, it twas a brother I had, but never known," whispered Flann, not believing his own words.

"And a big family it 'tis at home Flann."

"Home?" The words sounded as distant as Ireland was from Washington Heights. "And where might that be, Tomas?"

"Now 'tis County Kerry. I own a shop makin' the finest saddles in Europe. And didn't I find myself a bride? I'm the father of three sons, your nephews. And your three grandnieces and two grandnephews."

A bride. The words took Flann back to the early days in New York City. Once again, he could see his Dwiggy. "Twas' married myself once, for a short while and then... "

"Flann," said Big Jim, "let me be on my way. For sure, you and your brother have a lot of catchin' up to do. It's a miracle. It truly is."

29

The Freeze was all but forgotten and was replaced by June showers, which cleansed 177th street. The torrents of water carried fleets of Popsicle stick rafts, chased after by children, toward thirsty sewer drains. Once more, the asphalt became a freshly washed blackboard and a clean slate for Indian chalk artists.

Kate sat beneath the shadow of the chimney, safe from the tarpaper that held onto the heat of the day. She closed her law dictionary, the new one her parents had given her for Christmas, content with having reached letter *V. Vexata quffisito: from the Latin; a question often agitated or discussed, but not determined or settled.*

The previous graduation ceremony had gone as planned, and it had surprised no one when Sister Mary of the Crucifix announced that Kate won the Medal for Overall Excellence, for the eighth consecutive time. Her valedictorian speech reminisced about the past eight years and the future challenges the class of 1963 would undoubtedly face.

Kate removed the Eleventh Commandment sign from her door, which warned Danny about bursting into her room, before he came home from the hospital. He was free to come and go, she had no plans to post a new sign on her room in Hicksville. She packed her possessions in the boxes Danny and Rory had brought home from the A&P. Melinda and her stuffed friends found a temporary home in the arts and crafts box atop the cop shirt smock. Jack Kennedy's campaign buttons and the Ricky Nelson magazine pictures shared a shoebox. Liam thought the Nancy Drew novels, each read twice by his daughter, would make a nice addition to the Incarnation School library. Kate responded by placing the books in a box and writing in large block letters, KATE'S ROOM as her father watched.

Colleen had been busy too. She carefully wrapped the Dunn Christmas ornaments in newspaper, paying special attention to the Wishing Bench and the bookmarker, while thinking about those days after Danny came home from the hospital. She remembered the presents that waited under The Tree. Danny loved the ping-pong ball space gun from Rory and another platoon of toy soldiers from Grandma and Grandpa that reinforced the regiment stationed in the toy chest. His big surprise present was a castle with knights on horseback. The gift tag said it came from Saint Nicholas but Danny remembered seeing the same castle in the window of Hobby Land, which added to the doubts he began to feel about Santa's toy factory.

Colleen and Nora enjoyed their bottles of toilet water and Liam's new shaving cup impressed him. The football cards Kate bought yielded three Giants players and that brought a smile to her brother's face. A New York Giant jacket was Rory's big gift, one that he did not remove until the temperature in Washington Heights broke sixty-five degrees. Shannon received art supplies so she would not have to smuggle them home from school, water colors from Rory, her own numbered pencils from her aunt and uncle, and tons of paper and an easel from Grandma and Grandpa.

The gift with the fancy bow turned out to be a coat with a price tag on it from Alexanders Department Store. The note said it was from Dad, but Shannon recognized her mother's handwriting. She was grateful for the coat and hoped that maybe next year Ernie would be Dad.

Kate had no idea what was in the large box from Rory propped up against the TV. She let Danny help her unwrap it, which was a Christmas tradition in apartment thirty-one. It was the telescope from Hobby Lands window she secretly wished for. An amazing gift that impressed the entire Dunn family.

The monsignor offered a Mass of Thanksgiving, and just about all of Washington Heights seemed to attend. Grandma attended in her coat that had a new matching set of buttons, which pleased her daughter. Grandpa proudly wore his new Irish sweater, a gift sent by Connor and Maria after they returned to the West Coast. Flann sat next to Miss H. Wellington Grimes proud of the Straw Spider chest recipients who filled the church and kept their pledges. Their wishes granted concerning Danny, they placed their chests at the manger, so many that the Magi, could no longer see the Holy Family.

■ ■ ■

The prospect of viewing Saturn with the telescope drew closer as the sky over Washington Heights darkened. The ringed planet had been in position the past five nights, but a cloud cover blew from the west, concealing the sky. Kate smiled as Venus appeared, as always, the emcee for the astronomical performance about to begin. The newspaper said what she already had learned from Saturday's seminar at the Hayden Planetarium. The northwestern sky would be the stage for Saturn.

"Any seats left?" asked Rory walking toward Kate.

"One, you're in luck," said Kate upbeat.

Rory watched his sister maneuver the telescope. She had become adept at setting it up and mastered quickly how to follow the rapid movement of the stars by turning the arm attached to the axis. There were changes Rory had observed in Kate since she blown out the thirteen candles on her birthday cake two months ago, like the touch of lipstick he watched her apply before she went out and the rollers in her hair that Danny made fun of.

"So, do we finally get to see Saturn tonight, Kate?" asked Rory.

"Everything looking AOK. That's NASA talk," said Kate half-jokingly.

"Do you think they'll do it Kate?"

"Do what?" Kate replied as she adjusted the eyepiece.

"Go to the moon and back, like President Kennedy said."

"I sure do believe it. The moon, and then someday a spaceship that lands like an airplane. That's what they say at the planetarium."

"You're going to do great things at Hicksville High School, Kate," said Rory.

"Right now, I'd just like to get focused on Saturn. I'm a little early, should be in about thirty minutes, but I'm sure it'll be worth the wait. So stick around, I think you're going to enjoy this."

"No, I mean it Kate. I think you're going to do important stuff in your life, really important things, things that will make a difference." said Rory.

He watched as Kate made miniscule adjustments to the telescope while the sky darkened and the stars obediently returned.

"So are you Rory. We all know you're going to be a great football player, and after that, you can do anything you want," said Kate.

"I'm not going to be a great football player, Kate. Sometimes I think I'm not going to be great at anything."

"Sorry, buddy, but you already are great. And I happen to know that if you put your mind to it, you can accomplish anything you want."

"I'm too small," said Rory, barely above a whisper.

"What?" said Kate in disbelief.

"I'm too small to play in Division One or Two," Rory chuckled. "And all this time you thought you were the only one with a size issue."

"Dad thinks you're going to play for Notre Dame," said Kate, still shocked.

"All Irish fathers want their sons to play for Notre Dame."

"So, where will you play? Because you have to play, and I know how much you love the game."

"Oh, don't worry, I'll play in some small college. Might even get a partial scholarship ... maybe Iona. They have a pretty good Division Three team."

"You know I'll be going to your games. And what about after that Rory? What would you like to do?"

" There is so much out there. But teacher, I was thinking. Then I could coach high school ball somewhere. I think I would like that. What about you?"

"I won't be going to SHM that's for sure. But, I can still go to Marymount College." Kate had resigned herself to the situation regarding the move; Danny surviving the fall was what mattered. Everything else seemed trivial compared to life without her little brother.

"I don't know about that." Kate spun around at the sound of her father's voice, thinking that her going to college had become a problem.

"Hi Dad!" said Rory to their father, wondering what was in the box he carried.

Mary followed behind Liam, next to Colleen, who held Danny's hand. "Any sign of Saturn yet?" asked Colleen.

"Not yet," replied Kate, eying the box.

Mary's nose stopped running, on schedule, two days before Easter, so there were no tissues protruding from her pockets. She wore the same expression that covered her face when she had exciting news to share with her best friend.

"Here you are Kate … a graduation present," said Liam.

Kate opened the box, revealing a white blazer with the SHM logo.

"I… I don't understand," said Kate, bewildered.

"Kate," said Liam, "we know how much you wanted to attend SHM and how hard you worked."

"But we are moving and …"

"The train leaves Hicksville at six-thirty in the morning and arrives at Penn Station at seven-fifteen. The A train will take you to 207th street. Plenty of time to get to school. You earned a full scholarship, so you also earned a train ticket. If you want to go to SHM, you can. Not going to be easy, but yours if you want it." said Liam happily.

Kate slipped into the blazer. It fit her perfectly, which meant her mother had been busy with a needle and thread.

"You look great, Kate," said Danny.

"What do you say, Kate? Ready to be the youngest commuter out of Hicksville?" asked Colleen.

"And the smartest," added Danny.

"Speech! Speech!" said Rory kiddingly.

"Yes, I am ready and I will make you all proud. I promise you that," said Kate.

30

The three-car convoy drew little attention as it entered Gate of Heaven Cemetery. Black vehicles were forever arriving and advancing on gravesites where funeral directors waited for their customers. They drove on a twisting road, past the original graves occupied years earlier. Forgotten now, they lacked the Christmas wreaths that covered the tombstones on fresher graves. The lead car pulled into a parking area where three muddied backhoes sat behind a white fence, discretely hidden from view. The remaining cars continued, obediently obeying the five mile-per-hour speed limit.

The doors of a black Tahoe opened with preplanned precision. The four occupants of the vehicle exited in the same fashion. They did not wear uniforms, but were dressed in identical black suits. They were tall men with broad shoulders who opted for short-cropped, military-style haircuts.

A dusting of snow had fallen three hours before sunrise. Brown, dormant grass vanished and was replaced by a fresh whiteness that added a pleasant wintry crack to the air. Two of the men approached the limousine while their colleagues strategically positioned themselves on the road. The driver of the limousine exited first. He was somewhat shorter than the others were but appeared just as fit, with the same haircut and black suit.

He slid his hand under his arm and adjusted the modified sixteen-round Glock into a more comfortable position. His head slowly turned, scanning the area like a periscope hunting for prey. He paid little attention to the small gathering of mourners, knowing the security detail would keep their attention focused on that distant gravesite.

The driver opened the rear door, and another Secret Service agent stepped out, followed by Associate Justice of the United States Supreme Court Katherine Dunn.

"There are boots in the trunk, Madame Justice."

"No need, Patrick, not that much of a snow, but certainly nice this time of year. Wouldn't you agree?"

"Yes, I would. Very nice, Judge."

Kate consumed a deep breath and savored it before exhaling. Her perfectly tailored blue suit allowed for a quarter inch of her beige silk blouse to trim each sleeve. Her silver hair brushed her collar and offered itself without the aid of artificial color. She wore glasses that some in the media considered a tad oversized, and that had the slightest tint. Pinned to her lapel was the miniature diamond spider she attached to every garment she wore except for her judicial robe.

Kate could see the gravesite from the roadside. A sapling planted decades earlier that had grown into a towering oak tree served as a beacon. The undisturbed snow protested and crunched under Kate's feet as she made her way to the grave.

She moved with the athletic flair of a woman ten years younger. Pursuant to protocol, the two Secret Service agents followed Kate, but then paused, allowing her to approach the grave in privacy. A flock of startled sparrows, like those frolicking birds on the fire escape of apartment thirty-one sprang from the tree, which stubbornly held on to a few dead leaves.

Kate placed the small Christmas tree she had brought with her in front of the stone and stepped back. The name Dunn was grit blasted on it in large letters, along with the words, *Beloved Son Rory. Killed in Action Vietnam, May 12, 1969.*

Colleen's parents lived to see Kate graduate from law school. Shortly after Kate passed the bar exam Grandpa Finn died of a stroke. Grandma Bridget moved into the house in Hicksville and passed away peacefully in her sleep five years later.

After the loss of Rory, Colleen never again laughed. She smiled politely when required, but she never again laughed. She joined Rory in 1987 after refusing the chemotherapy that would have prolonged her life. The Wishing Bench disappeared. Kate never asked her mother about it. She thought that one day she would place it on her own tree, but she never found it.

Liam only spoke when spoken to after Rory's death. He died of heart attack seven months after Colleen passed away, holding the Zippo lighter that had survived the war with him. His pre-planned funeral arrangements called for no church service. The two Purple Hearts and the Navy Cross awarded to him and that appeared in his wedding portrait with Colleen were missing when Danny looked for them in the attic. The medals, like the bench, had vanished.

During July and August, when the court recesses, Kate retreats to her summer residence on Greenwood Lake with her husband, Frank Romano from 172nd street. They had gone years without seeing each other and then reunited at a judicial symposium at Fordham Law School; he had become an attorney too. Frank had his knee blown out in his first year at Notre Dame, which ended his football career but also kept him out of the army.

Deputy Inspector Danny Dunn, NYPD, bought a summer place of his own in Wah Ta Wah Park, just down the road from his sister. He sails the lake on a boat he named *Linen Angel* with his wife Jane, and their children, Rory, and Erin.

Shannon spends two weeks with her cousin every summer. In the early-morning hours, when the light is unspoiled and as fresh as the dew, she paints. Her works are on display in the Metropolitan Museum of Art and throughout Europe. Children, the world over are the benefactors of her generosity. Her husband died in a car crash when Shannon was thirty-one and pregnant with her son Nathaniel, who later became a pediatric surgeon. She never remarried.

Ernie went on to be Dad after he returned from rehab and remained Dad for the rest of his life. He died sober in 1997. He never returned to Nora, who married a coworker at the insurance company they worked for. She went on to have a comfortable life and died at the age of eighty-one.

Mary Garvey Murry became a New York City schoolteacher and married a firefighter. She continues to blow her nose from Halloween to Easter and spends the entire summer with her best friend on the lake.

Flann McFarland lived to his eighties. The monsignor of Incarnation Church honored Flann's wish and buried him with Dwiggy at Gate of Heaven Cemetery. He visited his brother in Ireland every Christmas for the rest of his life. His friend, Miss Grimes, moved out in the middle of the night and left behind everything except the cotton candy machine. No one ever knew how old she was or where she went.

Dusk remains Kate's favorite time at the lake, sitting by a fire, watching the sun slip beneath the rolling hills of Sterling Forest, contently listening to her son, James, an architect, read a story to Jack her grandson, resting on his mother's lap.

Alone, after the others drift off to sleep, Kate gazes at her stars with the telescope Rory gifted her on that last Christmas in Washington Heights. She walks the staircase in her mind and once more returns to the roof of 650, where Rory waits. Together again, they listen to their mother recite her psalm as Liam places the gold star atop The Tree. A little to the left, Liam. No, a little to the right. Yes, Liam, that's perfect.

THE END

AFTER THOUGHTS

A special thanks to my wife Helen, who shared me with the Dunn family the past three years with patience and understanding. Her keeping me focused when I wondered off in different directions proved invaluable. Helen, changed my life when she entered it, and our journey together has been nothing short of amazing. To my daughter Jeneen, and my son Jason, I hope I didn't embarrass you. Thanks to Toni Astor, who tamed the tsunami I presented her with. Her suggestions and input were priceless. A heartfelt thankyou to the entire team at CreateSpace who bring words to readers that might otherwise have gone unheard.

As the reader perhaps guessed, I grew up in Washington Heights. In 1965, we moved to the Inwood section of Manhattan. Our building was across the street from The Academy of the Sacred Heart of Mary. The school was well known to me. A family member, Elaine Santo Carlo attended the school. She went on to graduate from Marymount College and became a New York City school teacher.

In 1967, Consolidated Edison Company was in a hiring frenzy, as many of the men who worked in the trenches, were retiring. Most, with close to 50 years in the trench. A golden opportunity, for a kid who wasted four years at George Washington High School. Later, I went on to become a partner at JP&R Legal Advertising Agency in lower Manhattan. Not being an attorney, I became good friends with *Black's Law Dictionary,* as did Kate Dunn. William Mannion, my partner for twenty-two years remains at the agency, which continues to thrive.

I served in Vietnam, as a nineteen-year-old infantryman, with the 7th Squadron 17th Air Cavalry. When I first visited the Vietnam Veteran's Memorial in Washington DC, I watched the visitors walk past the names memorialized on The Wall.

I wanted, so very much, to tell them about the men I had served with, strangers to the tourists on that hallowed ground. I hope that I have honored their memory with my words and that the reader can sense the loss that families, like the Dunn family, came to endure.

I chose the name Done, sorry Dunn, because the era, in which The Freeze takes place, has long since recessed into history. For those who sipped an egg cream, swung a broomstick bat, or walked beneath those glorious Christmas lights that spanned across urban roadways, I hope you enjoyed a trip home. For the younger reader, I hope you enjoyed your visit to Washington Heights and will remember Rory and his family. And, to each of you, may your Straw Spider wishes come true, now, and always.

RDB

ABOUT THE AUTHOR

Ron DeBoer used his own life experiences as the inspiration for his new historical novel, *The Freeze*. DeBoer spent his childhood in Washington Heights and now lives with his wife, Helen, on the Jersey Shore.

Made in the USA
Middletown, DE
07 May 2020

93233653R00116